ABOUT THE AUTHOR

Dr. Frank Y. Panol is also the author of the book–*Go Green at Home: Save money by saving energy and the environment.* He is an engineer by training, agricultural development specialist by profession and environmentalist in practice. He graduated *magna cum laude* from Central Luzon State University in the Philippines and was an East-West Center scholar at the University of Hawaii, USA. Dr. Panol holds a Ph.D. in agricultural engineering from Michigan State University, USA. He was an adjunct faculty at Texas State University where he lectured on Business Statistics and Production and Operations Management. At Middle Tennessee State University, Dr. Panol taught Quantitative Research Methods and Information Management Systems.

He served as director for research and development and assistant vice president for agribusiness at Victorias Milling Company in the Philippines, formerly the world's biggest integrated sugar milling and refining facility. Dr. Panol was an Asian Development Bank consultant evaluating progress and accomplishments of ADB-funded agricultural research projects in Asia. He coordinated for the Philippine government the planning and preparation of a $41 million integrated rural infrastructure development project funded by the World Bank.

SUPER RING

DR. FRANK Y. PANOL

Order this book online at www.trafford.com
or email orders@trafford.com

Most Trafford titles are also available at major online book retailers.

Print information available on the last page.

ISBN: 978-1-4907-2697-7 (sc)
ISBN: 978-1-4907-2699-1 (hc)
ISBN: 978-1-4907-2698-4 (e)

Library of Congress Control Number: 2014902093

Because of the dynamic nature of the Internet, any web addresses or links contained in
this book may have changed since publication and may no longer be valid. The views
expressed in this work are solely those of the author and do not necessarily reflect the
views of the publisher, and the publisher hereby disclaims any responsibility for them.

Any people depicted in stock imagery provided by Thinkstock are models,
and such images are being used for illustrative purposes only.
Certain stock imagery © Thinkstock.

Trafford rev. 04/13/2015

 www.trafford.com
North America & international
toll-free: 1 888 232 4444 (USA & Canada)
fax: 812 355 4082

Dedication

It gives me the greatest pleasure to dedicate this book to my grandson, Nathaniel M. Panol. He made Jay and Ellen happy parents and ensured the continuance of my father Bonifacio's progeny.

Acknowledgement

I thank my wife, Dr. Zeny Sarabia-Panol, for her editing of this book. She is Associate Dean and Professor in the College of Mass Communication at Middle Tennessee State University. She is also the immediate past editor of the *International Communication Research Journal*, a publication of the International Communication Division, Association for Education in Journalism and Mass Communication.

Germane support selflessly provided by my children, Jay and wife Ellen, M.A. Caesar, Minnette and Ace is deeply appreciated and gratefully acknowledged. It made completing and getting the book published much less arduous.

Table of Contents

CAMANOR AND LAWA 1

Year 2050. The decade before reaching the mid-21st century has been characterized by great social turmoil and disastrous natural events worldwide. Unabated global warming and the resulting climate change brought about extreme weather conditions such as increased frequency of hurricanes and floods of biblical proportions that killed millions of people and destroyed infrastructure vital to the economy. More frequent and unseasonal strong tornadoes occurred in areas not ordinarily along their paths and wrecked havoc to communities hit. Severe droughts and high temperatures in some areas greatly increased the occurrence of hard-to-control destructive wildfires.

Also in the past decade, more frequent volcanic eruptions that spewed in the atmosphere several billion tons of fine ash particles and caused acid rain have affected the health of people in several continents.

Moreover, high-magnitude earthquakes brought about by continuing continental drift and the clashing of tectonic plates have destroyed several nuclear power plants, directly or by tsunamis, setting loose deadly radiation in Europe, Asia, the Americas and other areas.

As a consequence, the general health of the world population declined despite advances in medicine. World order, if there was any, became chaotic. All sorts of crime involving human victims went global.

The story of the Super Ring is about fighting a despicable crime committed against residents of a peaceful community, Camanor, whose only sin is the good health of most of its people.

Camanor is a centuries-old town with a population of nearly 8,000, of which 80 percent are descendants of the once powerful Sabang native tribe. A farming community engaged in cattle ranching, wheat, corn and vegetable production, it is a thriving and peaceful rural town. Blessed with rich soil, desirable topography and a strong social bond among residents, Sabang has maintained all its important ancient tribal traditions.

Vital among Camanor's blessings is Lawa, a giant cavern, which has a natural underground lake. The cavern and lake cover a total area of 600 acres, 450 acres of which is hard level ground while 150 acres form the underground lake that ranges in depth from a few feet along the edges to nearly 100 feet at the center. This natural subterranean formation evolved some 25 million years ago when ground water slowly dissolved the limestone layer and left on the top the hard igneous rocks, primarily granite.

Lawa is situated 300 feet below ground level. It is accessible through a paved walkway for able-bodied persons willing to walk and through a passenger elevator for disabled persons, the elderly, those with young children and those who are just not willing to walk. Water temperature in the lake is constant at 84°F year-round making it an ideal recreational spot particularly for swimming and row boating.

This natural gem serves the community in many ways. It is a park of some sort where people congregate for recreation and pleasure and where tribal meetings on important issues are held. It is a playground large enough for many sports competitions. It is a religious place where regular weekly service is held. Most of all, Lawa provides a shelter where people seek refuge from tornadoes, radiation released by destroyed nuclear power plants, from fine volcanic ash particles circling the atmosphere as well as acid rain. It is Lawa that has protected and kept the people of Camanor relatively healthy during the past tumultuous decade that also saw increased ultra violet radiation resulting from ozone depletion in the atmosphere.

As a religious place, Lawa is significant in that it is believed the spirits of powerful tribal ancestors reside in the cavern and could be called upon for help when the tribe is in grave danger. Legend has it that twice in the last century these spirits helped the tribe ward off land grabbers wanting to take over their fertile farmlands with support of local bandits posing as members of the U.S. military. Many members of the tribe would have been massacred had it not for the intercession of the spirits.

RANDOM KIDNAPPING 2

In early March 2050, reports of missing persons in Camanor started to pile up in the Police Department's office. And as days wore on the number of people reported missing alarmingly increased. For instance, by the third week of March, two persons were reported missing. Before the end of March there were already four being sought by family members and by the first week of April, the total number of missing persons already rose to six.

The missing seem to be abducted at random as there was no pattern in terms of age, gender and status in life nor the time of their disappearance. Amy, a vivacious fourth grader, who never missed to smile at people she met on her way to and from school not far from her home, failed to return home in the afternoon of March 19. Edgar, a point guard in the Sabang High School basketball team failed to report for an important practice Saturday morning of March 22, while Josie who works part-time as a waitress at a local restaurant was last seen coming out of the joint at closing time the evening of Friday, April 3. The randomness of the disappearances baffled the police. Young students, employees, adults, street guys, plain housewives, etc. simply vanished. This being the first time it ever happened in Camanor, threw the entire community on edge. The community never had a problem of such magnitude until now.

Maintenance of peace and order as well as the general safety and security of the residents of Camanor rest on the shoulders of Police Chief Joshua Dean and nine other police officers composed of six males and three females. Chief Dean, a former Navy Seal and Iran war veteran, has occupied the position for more than three years now after he was elected Police Chief by a landslide vote.

For four generations the community has entrusted their safety and security to the Dean family. Joshua's great-great grandfather was chief of the Sabang tribe. He was successful in uniting warring Sabang factions. His great grandfather and later his grandfather succeeded as tribal chief by tradition. When tribal tradition was replaced by democratic election to the position, Joshua's father was elected for two 4-year terms until his retirement three years ago when Joshua became police chief.

Joshua is a devoted family man with a 17-year old son – Nathan and a 9-year old daughter – Eriga. Nathan, who just recently got his non-professional driver's license is quarterback of Camanor High School's football team while Eriga plays in the elementary school's soccer team. Both Nathan and Eriga excel academically aside from being topnotch athletes. Joshua's wife, Mayfair, works with a bank in Camanor.

In this ever peaceful community, people are happy and always trustful of each other. But the recent mysterious disappearances of some residents are casting a dark shadow in the town's nearly 300 years of existence.

Joshua called a town hall meeting to inform the town council and everyone of recent developments. With the concurrence of town officials, the Police Department proposed steps to address with utmost urgency the problem of soaring number of disappearances in the community. These include, among others, deputizing select individuals to augment the police force when needed, posting private lookouts in key locations throughout the town, having neighborhood watch volunteers and increased patrol and street visibility of the policemen. Most importantly, the town's people were asked to be vigilant about their surroundings. They also were encouraged to report any suspicious incident.

There is now strong cooperative efforts among the people to prevent further disappearance of Sabang residents. The Police Department under Police Chief Joshua Dean has doubled its street patrol particularly during rush hours and at dusk.

ABDUCTION OF POLICE CHIEF 3

In the afternoon of the day following the town hall meeting, police headquarters received a report of a suspicious vehicle that looked like a giant recreational vehicle or RV. The report came as a video feed shown in the police station's monitor simultaneously as it was being taken by a Sabang family riding in a car passing in the opposite direction as the RV. According to the recorded voice, the suspicious RV-looking vehicle was parked at the shoulder of a state highway four miles away from the Camanor plaza, which is the center of the town. As can be seen in the video, a white passenger van with heavily tinted windows was parked alongside the RV and appeared to be transferring two hooded passengers into it.

Alarmed by what he saw in the video report, Chief Dean opened the firearms cabinet and took out two M-16B assault rifles and boxes of ammunition. He gave

one to his patrol partner, Officer Kyle Demos. "Let's go
and try to catch up with that suspicious RV," Joshua told
Officer Demos. They left quickly. Officer Demos took the
wheel. With siren blaring and warning blue and red lights
flashing, Joshua's patrol car reached the reported site in
time before the suspicious RV with motor engine already
running could pull out.

Officer Demos stopped the patrol car in front of
the RV to prevent it from moving forward. Chief Dean
alighted and motioned the driver to come down from the
RV. Officer Demos then slowly backed up the patrol car
and parked on the side of the road about 25 feet from the
rear of the RV. He watched intently with the barrel of the
M-16B resting on the dashboard.

"Is there a problem Officer," asked the driver in
gargling, nervous tone.

"Mister, I have a video report showing a white van
alongside your RV in this location transferring what
appears to be hooded persons," replied Chief Dean. "You
know that is unsafe and illegal," Chief Dean continued.
"And those individuals being transferred, why were they
hooded?"

"Nothing of that sort occurred here, Officer,"
answered the driver.

"I want to see those individuals, so please open this door," said Chief Dean pointing to the driver side passenger door.

"There is nothing to see Officer," replied the driver in an apparent delaying tactic.

"Open the door now or I will," insisted Chief Dean, who is now visibly irritated.

"I will not do that if I were you Officer," the driver warned.

Suddenly the door slowly opened and almost simultaneously the driver, who had repositioned himself behind Chief Dean, pushed him hard inside the RV rendering him imbalanced. A stocky man apparently waiting inside grabbed Chief Dean and with help of two other men pricked a syringe needle on his exposed lower neck. With the tingling sensation in his neck, which was fast spreading to his upper torso, Chief Dean immediately realized he had been tranquilized. Wanting to let Officer Demos know what had happened and hoping he could save him, Chief Dean summoned what was left of his adrenaline and consciousness and forced his way out of the door, ramming and knocking down the driver outside of the RV. Both men slumped on the pavement beside the vehicle. The three men from inside the RV including the stocky man with the tranquilizer syringe rushed outside the RV and lifted Chief Dean back inside the vehicle. The driver reentered the RV as well.

Just as Officer Demos got his patrol car moving toward the RV to rescue Chief Dean, a radio-controlled 50-mm caliber machine gun popped out of the RV's back door and fired at the police car hitting the hood and both front tires. Officer Demos was hit in the leg and lost control of his patrol car that eventually fell into a 40-foot ravine by the roadside. Officer Demos was able to eject from the burning car before it hit the ground and exploded. He also was able to tell headquarters what was happening including the abduction of Chief Dean.

An antidote to the tranquilizer was presumably administered on Chief Dean because police headquarters received a distress signal from him minutes after he was brought inside the RV. At least they were certain Chief Dean was alive although they didn't know where he was and who abducted him.

Two police cars with three heavily-armed officers each rushed to the site followed by EMS ambulance and a fire truck. The RV was gone when the responders arrived at the site where Chief Dean was abducted.

One patrol car tried to follow the RV but they could not determine whether the RV continued on the state highway or exited to the interstate and in which direction. Without concrete leads, they turned back. However, they alerted state troopers, who may be in either direction of the interstate.

The other responders concentrated on the burning car and searched for Officer Demos. He was found unconscious under a thick bush and tall grasses. Aside from the machine gun shot wound on his leg, Officer Demos sustained two broken ribs after he jumped out of the burning car. The paramedics quickly brought him to the hospital for treatment. Officer Demos underwent several procedures on his broken ribs and leg wound.

Meanwhile, Police Deputy Ronald Sturgess carefully assessed the event as it unfolded when he was informed of the condition of Officer Demos. He was certain this was connected to the series of disappearances and kidnapping of several Sabang people. What worried him most was the abduction of Police Chief Joshua Dean. Deputy Sturgess immediately informed the town mayor by phone about the latest development.

Naturally, the situation further increased the weariness among the already-jittery populace. Fewer people are now seen in the streets after dusk. Municipal officials knew this was disastrous for business. But of course there is little that could be done about it. Deputy Sturgess thought that only the safe return of Police Chief Dean and the ultimate dismantling of the kidnapping syndicate can normalize life in Camanor.

PROFILING THE KIDNAPPERS 4

*T*he abduction of Police Chief Joshua Dean had the entire town worried of his and their safety. Police Deputy Sturgess immediately informed Mayfair, Chief Dean's wife, who was going home from work for the day. She called to pick up Eriga, who in turn told Nathan about what had happened particularly the abduction of their father.

Instead of directly going home, Nathan went to the police headquarters to learn more about the incident. He requested to view the video taken by Officer Demos as well as the earlier video report of the passing car. Nathan meticulously scrutinized both videos viewing them in several angles and running them at different speeds. It was as if Nathan was trying to understand the profile of the abductors, their motives and the nature of their operation, etc.

Nathan knew that Officer Demos would have plenty of insights into the group that abducted Joshua. Together with another police officer, Nathan proceeded to the hospital where Officer Demos has just came out of the operating room and still under heavy sedation with life support system connected to his body.

"Good afternoon Doctor," Nathan greeted the surgeon in-charge of Officer Demos. "I am Nathan, son of Police Chief Dean, who had been abducted this afternoon," Nathan introduced himself to the surgeon. "I would like very much to have a brief word with Officer Demos because my father will be in grave danger if we do not do something immediately," Nathan continued.

"I understand," replied the doctor very considerately. "Let me check the vital signs of the patient to see if he can talk even for a short time."

"Thank you Doctor," acknowledged Nathan as the surgeon entered the ICU where Officer Demos was. After a minute or so the doctor through the glass wall motioned Nathan and the police officer to enter the ICU.

"Hi Officer Demos," greeted Nathan.

"Hi Nathan," replied Officer Demos in a very low voice. He has known Nathan for quite sometime already as Chief Dean often took him along in police camps and other field exercises. Officer Demos also has a son of Nathan's age whom he took along in these outdoor activities.

"Sorry to disturb you in your condition," Nathan started the conversation. "I just want to get your thoughts on what we are up against with my father's abductors and presumably the kidnapper of several of our town's people."

Officer Demos did not speak for a couple of minutes as if trying to gain strength to be able to say what was in his mind. Then in a shaky, halting voice slowly said, "They appear to be a big, well-organized professional group, heavily armed with sophisticated modern weaponry and ruthlessly working outside the law and I mean really ruthless." Officer Demos paused for few seconds and continued, "We have to move fast but with great caution. Police Chief Dean's life is in great danger. The heavily - tinted white van that supposedly transferred the two hooded passengers to the suspect RV may still be in Camanor to kidnap more victims." Officer Demos spoke with authority and measured certainty.

"Do you recall how many people were in the van?" Nathan inquired.

"I actually did not see the van or the people in it. It just left when we arrived at the scene. But from my observation on how their operation is structured, I would guess only two or at most three people," Officer Demos replied. "But, I tell you they are ruthless," he continued.

Nathan held Officer Demos' left hand and said, "Thank you Officer Demos; you have been most helpful. I wish you fast recovery."

After thanking the surgeon, Nathan and the police officer left.

UNDER THE OAK TREE 5

*N*athan phoned his mother, Mayfair, to tell her that he was on his way home after gathering information from the police headquarters and from talking briefly with Officer Demos. Mayfair and Eriga are both anxiously awaiting Nathan home for more details. They of course wanted to know what could be done to rescue Joshua.

As soon as she heard Nathan's car park on the driveway, Eriga rushed out to meet him. With tears in her eyes, she embraced Nathan and asked, "What will happen to our father?"

"We have to think about it," replied Nathan feeling sorry that he could not be more definite and assuring to Eriga regarding Joshua.

"Dinner is ready," called out Mayfair. "Let's eat so we can think well," she added.

Only the sound of forks and knives touching the plates could be heard at the dinner table. Nobody dared speak for fear of choking or crying. This was exactly what occurred when Mayfair picked up Eriga from her soccer practice. Dinner was quick and when it was over Nathan spoke. "Eriga kindly help mother with the dishes. After that, can the two of you please join me under the oak tree?"

"The dishes can wait, let's go and talk about the problem," Mayfair replied. She picked up her shawl from the master's bedroom and walked toward the oak tree. Eriga followed by her side while Nathan was a few steps in front.

The oak is a 400-year old tree in the front yard of the Dean's 150-year old ancestral home. Hardwood benches were built around the 6-foot diameter base where people sit for comfortable conversation or solitude. This was a favorite place for the Deans to tell stories and pass on to the new generation ancestral adventures and legends of the Sabang tribe. Nathan recalled his father telling him some years back what Joshua's father had told him about how the spirits of Sabang ancestors saved many members of the tribe from being massacred and robbed of their rich farmland by land grabbers supported by local bandits posing as the military. This story stuck in Nathan's young mind until now and he liked to keep recalling it over and over again.

When mother, son and daughter were seated on the wooden bench Nathan said, "Mother I have decided to seek help from the spirits of our Sabang ancestors. Father has told me stories about our ancestors helping the tribe in times of dire need. Please tell me whatever you could remember about how I can make contact with the spirits so I can ask for help in saving father and the rest of our town's people who have been kidnapped."

Mayfair did not have a ready answer for Nathan. She had to search hard for it. She looked up as if asking the oak tree for information. She then looked at Nathan and slowly spoke, "As far as I can recall, High Cloud was the greatest chief of the Sabang tribe. However, it was to all the spirits of the ancestors that plea for help was made. The spirit of High Cloud together with that of our other ancestors determined and decided the nature of help provided. High Cloud's spirit communicated with whoever was asking for help and confirmed as well as blessed the help being extended."

"But mother will the spirits listen to me?" asked Nathan. "I am just a kid, sort of, with no experience in what I planned to do," he continued. "They probably do not even know me."

"Speak from your heart with full seriousness and resolve," Mayfair answered. "The spirits know who you are by the blood that's flowing in your veins." She then added, "Our ancestors are wise and understanding. They will know what is best for the tribe."

"So it is in Lawa that I will speak to the spirits and ask for help," Nathan wanted to confirm from Mayfair what he has known all along from his father.

"Yes, at the sacred rock wall that has the carvings of our ancestors depicting various ancient war scenes as well as agricultural tools, farm animals and crops. It is in the sacred wall our tribe paid annual tribute in the form of native prayers, dances and various forms of celebration to honor our ancestors," Mayfair said.

Nathan himself has witnessed and participated with his family in several of these rituals that pay homage to the spirits. He knew what the atmosphere was during such celebrations. It was solemn yet festive.

"Lawa is still open and I want to go there now. Time is precious to us," Nathan said anxiously as he prepared to leave.

Mayfair gave him her blessings. "Good luck, my Son and let us know immediately the result. I will also make similar plea with the ancestors for you."

Eriga listened attentively to Nathan as Mayfair discussed the virtue and power of the spirits of Sabang ancestors and explored how to obtain help from them. Her curiosity had transformed into a strong desire to witness how communication with the spirits is done. But she is not sure whether her gender and age would prevent her from realizing such desire now. She should find out from Mayfair.

"Do they allow women in the spirit's home, Mother?" Eriga wanted to know. "Aside from being female, I am still really a girl."

"I am not sure about that Eriga," said Mayfair. "But as far as I can see, there is no reason why they won't," she added.

"Because Mother if they do, I would like to go with Nathan," Eriga enthused.

Nathan affirmingly interrupted, "I agree with Mother that there is no reason not to allow you, Eriga in the sanctuary of the Sabang spirits."

"May I go with Nathan then, Mother?" Eriga again asked.

"Go ahead," said Mayfair. "Try to learn something from it," she added.

Turning to Nathan, Eriga said, "I'm really glad to go with you." She and Nathan then walked toward his car.

"Come," Nathan slowed down and held Eriga by her left hand. "Thank you for giving me company."

HIGH CLOUD AND THE SUPER RING 6

*T*he drive to Lawa was a blur as Nathan was very anxious to speak to the Sabang spirits. Traffic to and from Lawa had also ebbed for the night. Nathan and Eriga entered through a narrow walkway to reach the sacred rock wall faster than using the elevator in going down.

Upon reaching the sacred rock wall, Nathan and Eriga stood quietly for a brief moment, hearts pounding in eager anticipation. Nathan spoke, "Oh, great spirits of Sabang ancestors, we come to plead for help. Our tribe is in grave peril from foes we do not know much about. Many of our people have been kidnapped. My father Joshua in whom our community depended for safety and security was abducted yesterday. Please help us to save them and stop these criminals from doing our people harm. With your help and guidance, I am respectfully offering myself to do whatever I can. Please, great spirits, I respectfully call upon thee through the spirit of Sabang's great leader, High Cloud for help."

Nathan stopped talking and though his plea was short he appeared drained from it. The atmosphere was solemn and a deafening silence engulfed the place. Eriga remained speechless but attentive. Minutes passed.

Suddenly a cracking sound from the stone door opening was heard. Slowly a three-foot section of the sacred rock wall opened outward and a transparent figure of a man, clearly a spirit, in full tribal attire appeared. Inside the sacred wall was a strong light that seemed to penetrate through the spirit making a clear shining frontal view of Nathan and Eriga standing in front of the door.

"I am High Cloud," the spirit spoke. "We heard about your predicament and we will help you. Come inside," High Cloud continued and motioned Nathan and Eriga to enter.

High Cloud said, "Nathan, pick up that ring on the crystal pedestal and wear it in your right middle finger. That is a Super Ring, which the Sabang spirits have treasured for several centuries. You need that to successfully accomplish what you want to do."

The main body of the Super Ring is platinum (Appendix A), an extremely rare metal, also called white gold. The Super Ring's shape is similar to a sports ring. The hoop or body is 3/16 inch at the bottom and widens to 3/4 inch toward the shoulder. An 8-carat octagonal-shape blue diamond measuring about 3/16 inch on each opposite side is mounted on top of the body. The blue diamond is flanked on two sides by one piece each of erbium, a rare earth element (Appendix B) currently applied in infrared lasers and fiber optic technology. The square erbium measuring 3/16 inch on each side is embedded on the platinum shoulder. The outer surface of the platinum body is inscribed with Sabang words and incantations and some minute engravings of arrowheads, hatchets, knives and other native symbols.

The Super Ring derives its power from the intersection of the magnetic fields of the platinum, blue diamond and the erbium. The intersection blessed by ancient Sabang spirits reflected in the inscribed incantations and various native symbols generates the power that is transferred to whoever wears the Super Ring as granted by High Cloud.

High Cloud turned to Eriga and said, "We admire your courage and your coming here tonight, young lady, but we will let your brother Nathan do the mission alone. Later, when you are old enough and it becomes necessary, we will also help and equip you accordingly." Eriga nodded respectfully without uttering a word. She understood and respected the wisdom of High Cloud. She was already happy to be allowed to enter the Sabang spirit's abode and to be acknowledged by High Cloud for joining Nathan.

When Nathan placed the Super Ring in his right middle finger, a mild electrical jolt seemed to pass through his body and he felt differently. High Cloud said to him, "Whoever wears the Super Ring with the blessings of the Sabang great spirits is bestowed the combined strength of five dozen buffaloes, the blinding speed of a rifle bullet, eyesight of an eagle, night vision of an owl and enhanced hearing of a deer. And because you carry the same Sabang blood as Joshua, you will be able to communicate briefly with each other telepathically. Just think of him with intense concentration and you will connect to his mind and he will respond. As you search for him, you will be aided by Eagle Spirit during daytime. Just call on him and look up in the sky for his whereabouts. Also, Nikandro, the blacksmith in Camanor, may still have stocks of Sabang ancient weaponry that you may be able to use. Remember too that Nikandro is a descendant of a Sabang interrogator family that could help you extract information from suspects."

Nikandro is a mysterious person as no one knows how old he is and whether he is a human being or part spirit. What is known is that he always stood behind the Sabang tribe in times of need.

Nathan thanked High Cloud and told him he will return the Super Ring as soon as Joshua is saved and the current peril to the Sabang people is over. High Cloud nodded and said, "Our spirits will always be with you."

On the way out of Lawa, Eriga kidded Nathan, "Don't walk too fast; I do not want to be left behind." She continued, "Mother will be thrilled."

At home Mayfair was eagerly awaiting the return of Nathan and Eriga. She was at the door as soon as she heard Nathan's car roar in the driveway.

It was Eriga who told Mayfair what transpired at Lawa including the powers given by High Cloud to Nathan through the Super Ring. Mayfair was ecstatic and so thankful to the spirits. Nathan is now deep in thought and focusing his mind on Joshua. Then Joshua called out his name, implying their telepathic connection.

"Father!" Nathan blurted to the pleasant surprise of both Mayfair and Eriga. "Are you all right? We are glad to know you are not harmed. I am coming to save you and the others."

Thanking Nathan, Joshua said, "Be careful, Son." The telepathic link, however, was suddenly broken because of a commotion at Joshua's end caused by an interference on the satellite signal and Joshua was unable to concentrate his thoughts.

SEARCH FOR THE TINTED VAN 7

*E*arly the following morning Nathan went to Nikandro's shop and talked about ancient Sabang weaponry as well as possible help in interrogating the suspects. He then set out to locate the tinted white van that supposedly transferred two hooded individuals to the giant RV. Officer Demos thought this van might still be in Camanor. He dropped by the police headquarters to inform them of his mission and to let Police Deputy Sturgess knew the spirits of Sabang ancestors are helping him. He also told him that he will contact him in case he needed assistance.

Going fast at invisible speed, Nathan scoured through parking lots of hotels, motels, inns, truck stops and similar establishments offering overnight accommodations. No white van that resembles Officer Demos' description was found. However, Nathan spotted a white van near the front of a known 24-hour grocery store. A man was preparing a small table beside the van for a quick sale of overstock assorted electronic devices such as cell phones, iPads, DVDs, video games and similar gadgets and accessories. Honing in on the van, Nathan saw that it was heavily tinted. There were two well-built men, one in red t-shirt and the other wearing a blue long sleeve shirt standing by the table outside the van. Nathan posted himself at a point far enough to avoid suspicion but close enough to observe everything that was actually going on in and around the van. A number of people of various ages are starting to congregate to look at the items now on the table. They are curious of the deeply marked-down prices.

Nathan could clearly see that both men manning the van were surreptitiously scrutinizing everyone that came by. Boyd, Nathan's teammate on the Camanor High football team stopped by the van and started browsing on the gadgets found on the table. After a while, the man in red t-shirt approached him, had a little talk and invited him inside the van purportedly to show more items.

Boyd entered the van first followed by the man in red t-shirt who closed the van door behind him. Nathan through his supernatural hearing power heard a groan as apparently the man in red t-shirt suddenly covered

Boyd's face particularly his nose with cloth soaked in chloroform. Boyd slammed on the floor of the van unconscious. The man in red t-shirt handcuffed, gagged, blindfolded and tied his feet to a post in the rear section of the van. Boyd is completely helpless. Whatever little noise that occurred inside the van was drowned by the music being played in the van. Besides, the people browsing for the quick sale were too busy to notice anything unusual.

From the grocery store out came Lauren carrying a couple of Gatorade bottles she picked up from the store on the way to her cheer leading practice. But first she headed toward the van curious of the announced quick sale. Lauren, a rare combination of beauty, brain, athleticism and unequal charm, is a top honor student and the star cheerleader for the Camanor High School football team. She and Nathan knew each other but not very well. Just the usual hi or hello whenever they meet. Secretly, however, Lauren idolized Nathan as a top-rated quarterback of the Camanor High football team and for bringing honor to the school with several football championship trophies. That being the case, Nathan felt differently this time when he saw Lauren approach the

van. Whether it was the anticipation of what was about
to befall her or a special caring for her, he was not sure.

Many of the people earlier browsing for the special
sale have left. There was hardly anybody around the van
by this time. Lauren was met by the man in blue long
long sleeve shirt as she neared the van. He said, "We
are ready to close shop, young lady. You are lucky to
catch us before we leave. The good items are inside
the van. Go inside and have a look," motioning Lauren
toward the door of the van.

When Lauren stepped inside the van, the man in
blue shirt followed and immediately shut the door behind
him. He did to her exactly what they did to Boyd, i.e., the
chloroform, the gag, handcuff, blindfold and feet tied to a
post in the rear section of the van. She could only groan
inaudibly in distress. Nobody around heard it except
Nathan, thanks to the Super Ring.

Nathan decided to wait for the van to move to a
point where there were no or only few people around
before he would take action in order to avoid too much
disturbance. When it passed between two parked
Goodwill store 18-wheeler cargo trucks, the van was less
visible from the public on two sides. Nathan made his
move and signaled the driver to stop. The man in blue

shirt driving the van instead accelerated intent on running over Nathan, who was standing right on its path.

Nathan stood firm, two arms stretched forward mustering all the strength the Super Ring bestowed on him. The combined strength of five dozen buffaloes stopped the van from moving forward with the rear tires just skidding on the pavement that has heated up and gave off the noxious smell of burning tires and asphalt.

The man in red shirt seated on the passenger side pulled out a baseball bat from the bottom of his seat and opened the passenger door to go down. Before he can fully open the door, Nathan slammed it back pinning him between the door. A quick karate chop on the base of his neck rendered the man instantly unconscious. Almost simultaneously, Nathan moved to the driver side of the van and grabbed the man in blue shirt before he can pull out a gun from under the dashboard. Also, a karate chop on the base of the neck disabled the man. Nathan easily handcuffed him and tied his legs together. He did the same to the man in red shirt, who was already starting to regain consciousness.

Lifting the two kidnapper-suspects each by the collar after opening the rear door of the van, Nathan shove them inside. He released Boyd and Lauren and tied the men in their places. Boyd was elated. But more so Lauren, who could not hold back kissing Nathan on the cheek as her way of thanking him for the rescue. Nathan's whole body seemed to tingle with the kiss.

"Boyd, I am dropping you and Lauren off to the police headquarters so you can report the incident. I will go to Nikandro's place to interrogate these two men," Nathan told Boyd and Lauren. "Meantime search the men for anything they may have in their possession. I suspect they may have electronic signaling device or cyanide capsule," Nathan continued. "Lauren, please help Boyd with the search but be very careful and hold the baseball bat in case they misbehave."

"Right on," Boyd happily obliged.

Lauren grabbed the baseball bat and said, "At your service, Nathan."

Boyd found a timepiece from the man in blue shirt that appeared out-of-the-ordinary. He also found one cyanide capsule from each of them. "These guys are willing to commit suicide to avoid revealing secrets of their operation or suffering torture during interrogation," Boyd commented. Nathan nodded in agreement.

At police headquarters, Boyd and Lauren alighted from the van. Nathan got out and talked to Deputy

Chief Sturgess, who is now in-charge in the absence of Chief Dean. He handed to the deputy the timepiece and cyanide capsules found from the two kidnapping suspects. After briefly examining the timepiece, Deputy Sturgess said, "This gadget has just sent a distress signal to their central command that has now disabled any communication to and from the van hence erasing any trace of their location. Nathan thanked him and asked for two police officers to follow him to Nikandro's blacksmith shop. He also borrowed several handcuffs and shackles as well as a video camera used for interrogation. Nathan also got the original copy of his deputation paper with the Camanor Police Force, which he has to carry for the duration of his mission.

Before leaving the police headquarters, Nathan briefed Nikandro by cell phone of what transpired in the van earlier and the cyanide capsule found from the two men. He told Nikandro he was on the way to his place with the two kidnapping suspects and two police officers, who were keeping an eye on the suspects and will be taking them back to police headquarters after the interrogation.

Nikandro said, "I will prepare my place for maximum effectiveness. You will keep the two men in separate rooms. We will first interrogate the man in blue shirt who appears to be the leader of the two. And if necessary we will also interrogate the other guy to cross check veracity of what they tell us. While waiting for my call they should not see each other nor hear any of the interrogation.

NIKANDRO'S PLACE 8

*N*athan drives the van with the two kidnapping suspects tied securely at its rear. The two police officers were in one patrol car following the van.

Nikandro meets Nathan and the officers when they arrived at his place.

Nikandro's place is composed of two buildings essentially separated by the driveway. On the north side is a 150-year old residential home where the family stays. On the south side is a blacksmith shop where farm tools, machete and other ancient Sabang weaponry for collectors are made. Occasionally the shop is also used specially in the olden days as interrogation venue by Sabang tribe leadership. This will be the first time after more than 100 years that the place will be used again for that purpose.

Nikandro led Nathan with the man in blue shirt still gagged, blindfolded, handcuffed and feet shackled to the room on the left side of the blacksmith shop. Inside the room the man was securely tied to a 4x4 wooden column extending from the ground to the ceiling. Nathan is guarding this suspect while waiting for Nikandro to call him.

Nikandro similarly guided the police officer with the kidnapper-suspect in red shirt to the room on the right side. This suspect is also securely tied to a 4x4 wooden column. One police officer is guarding him while waiting for Nikandro's call to interrogate. Nikandro also showed both Nathan and the police officer the way out from the rooms where the two men are held to the place for the interrogation.

The second police officer is now in the chamber mounting the video camera to record the interrogation process. Nikandro prepared the mounting location and position of the video camera. Although amazed at what he saw in the area, he was reserving any questions or comments until after the completion of the interrogation.

The entire compound was eerily quiet. Only the whizzing of air from the blower to the furnace can be heard. Some years ago a bellow supplied the air to the furnace. Nikandro has since modernized the equipment with the replacement of the bellow with electric blower thus freeing his hands from operating the bellow that required pushing and pulling its handle at regular interval to regulate the fire temperature in the furnace.

Suddenly a loud shriek and agonizing cry reverberated in the compound. It clearly emanated from Nikandro's interrogation chamber. The thought of unimaginable pain brought shivers to the two suspects. They started to perspire and became pale in anticipation of grave torture.

About 20 minutes after this, Nikandro called Nathan by cell phone. "Nathan, you can now bring your man to me. Before you take him out of the room, remove his blindfold and gag. Let him face the open door for about five minutes to acquaint his eyes to the bright light. Then slowly walk him toward the wooden bench in the middle where he will be seated. Walk him slowly so that he sees everything in the area."

Nathan did as Nikandro instructed. The first thing that caught the suspect's attention once his eyes have gotten used to the bright light is the furnace with glowing fire and Nikandro standing beside it looking at a metal shear that he just retrieved from the furnace, its cutting edges red hot. He took notice of it with fear. The more he perspired.

Nathan then walked him toward the bench where he will sit for interrogation. The bench is six feet long six inches wide and two inches thick of hard oak wood. It is supported at two ends by the same wood cut from the bench material. At one end of the bench near the furnace is a wooden head restraint that is flipped up. The suspect was seated straddling the bench with his feet tied together under the bench. His hands are still handcuffed at the back. Per Nikandro's instruction, the suspect was seated and tied a bit comfortably albeit temporarily anyway.

THE INTERROGATION 9

*T*he suspect in blue shirt protested, "You can not do this to me. I have protection by the law!" He perspired even more as he looked at the wash basin with fresh blood and what appeared to be the tip of a tongue submerged in three inches of water.

Nikandro quickly and forcefully replied. "You are breaking the law. You can not expect protection from it. But still, I will give you two choices. You can either talk and tell us all we want to know about your operation and face justice later on, or exercise your right to remain silent. If you do, I will make sure you remain silent for the rest of your life, assuming you live through it." Nikandro retrieved the iron shear from the fire and examined the tip making sure the suspect saw the red-orange glow of the shear. The suspect was visibly shaken as he contemplated his options in front of the furnace with Nikandro holding the red-hot shear. The splattered fresh blood in the interrogation area and what appears to be a freshly cut tip of a human tongue submerged in three inches of water in a wooden basin in front of the suspect further exacerbated his fears. For a while, the suspect can not get his eyes off the basin.

A moment of ghostly silence ensued. Nikandro then abruptly asked the suspect. "So which is it? Are you telling us what we want to know or not?" No response was heard. The suspect seemed confused and still unsure of what to do. The thought of life with a severed tongue and unable to talk to others, if he survived the ordeal was dueling against his loyalty toward his employer. He was shaking and perspiring profusely. Nikandro added more charcoal to the furnace, placed the shear again to the fire and switched the furnace blower on. The red-bluish fire intensifies.

After about three minutes, Nikandro turned to Nathan and said, "Nathan, strap him on the head restraint. Time to move along."

Nathan pushed the suspect toward the edge of the bench and flipped the wooden head restraint upward to a vertical position, ready to shackle the suspect into it. Suddenly the suspect spoke, "Stop, I'll talk!"

"That's better; you'll not regret it," Nikandro said reassuringly. He then switched the video on using its remote control. Nikandro's mounting of the video camera captures only the suspect's face and upper torso and excludes all other elements in the interrogation area. The suspect took a deep breath, showing sigh of relief.

Nikandro asked Nathan to transfer the handcuff from the back to the front of the suspect and to loosen the leg shackle. This makes the suspect more comfortable as he is able to move his feet more freely although still restrained.

"Okay then," Nikandro said. "Tell me your name, age, citizenship and position in this operation."

"Dexter Ruud, 40 years old, American citizen. I am in-charge of obtaining organ sources for the operation." The suspect promptly replied.

Nikandro nodded to Nathan signaling correctness of the name, citizenship and age based on the information from the driver's license taken from the suspect. Nathan smiled.

"What is your operation about?" Nikandro looking serious asked. This is the most important information they want to know.

"Our organization is registered as Nagro, Inc., which reads as Organ, Inc. in reverse. We are an organ harvester, that is, we gather all human organs such as lungs, heart, kidney, liver, pancreas, brain and others from live, healthy persons we kidnap. These organs are frozen and preserved using the latest technology and then sold in the international organ black market." Dexter, the suspect, showed equivocal pride in the uniqueness of their undertaking.

Both Nathan and Nikandro were shocked from what they heard. Nikandro continued questioning. "How is your operation able to conduct such a horrendous illegal trade internationally involving a heinous crime of killing healthy people and removing their organs?"

"Because of high demand and limited supply, many embassies have offered to facilitate the movement of the organs using their diplomatic pouches and other privileges. This is particularly so with rich countries where the health of their rich and influential citizens has greatly deteriorated as a consequence of global natural and human-caused catastrophes. In some countries, the drug cartels also want to be involved using their existing distribution infrastructure because of the prospect of big

money and the decreasing business in the drug trade."
Dexter now appears at ease in answering.

"How long has this operation been going on?"
Nikandro wanted to know.

"Very recent," Dexter declared. "There were problems at the beginning that needed to be ironed out foremost of which was the difficulty of recruiting doctors qualified and willing to extract all the organs from a living person. No American doctors are willing to do it. Qualified doctors not averse to the operation because of money have to be brought in from outside the United States."

Nikandro asked, "Where did you start this operation?"

Dexter hastily replied, "We started in the East. But after extracting organs from a dozen or so individuals it was determined that the general health condition of the people there was poor and we can not be assured of healthy organs. However, we were able to undertake successful and extensive dry-run of our operation including the trade of organs in the international black market. We moved our collection of organ sources to this place because of the excellent health record of Sabang people as determined by our research team. Accordingly, the Lawa where many of you spend recreational and religious time has provided protection to the people from all sorts of environmental risks like atmospheric fine ash from volcanic eruption, acid rain, ultra violet rays, nuclear fallout, cosmic radiation and other natural health hazards."

"If you are now getting the organ sources from Camanor, then your base of operation must be in this place." Nikandro's line of questioning is now trying to locate the whereabouts of abducted Police Chief Joshua Dean.

"No!" Dexter declared. "We do not have a permanent base. Our operation is totally portable. We move from one location to another depending on circumstances as determined by our chief of operation. Sometimes we are in an RV camping ground or in an abandoned municipal airport with vacant hangars or in vacated food processing facilities where our vehicles can park either outside or inside vacant warehouses."

Nikandro pressed on. "So where are your facilities located now and where do you keep the 'organ sources' that you have kidnapped?"

"I would not know the location of our facilities now because, as I said earlier, it keeps on moving from one place to another. This is possible because everything is done in what we call custom-built organ vehicle or OV," Dexter answered. "Organ sources are kept in custom-built organ vehicle referred to as organ source quarters or OV-SQ. There is an OV-OE, where organs are extracted. An OV-PG is another custom-built organ vehicle for plasma gasification, while an OV-SC is for security and communication. The OV-CC is the command center used by high-ranking officials and doctors performing the organ extraction together with other medical staff. The OV-SC is loaded with high-tech weaponry including high caliber machine guns, miniature helicopter drone and a sub-compact armored fighting vehicle (AFV), all radio-controlled. It has global positioning satellite (GPS)-radar connection to track intruders within its compound. Basically, OVs are giant RVs with the interior customized to serve the particular purpose.

Nathan wanted to know more about the OVs. "If they are all giant RVs, how do you distinguish one from the other?"

"It's not easy," said Dexter. But there are some external differentiating features. "For instance, the OV-PG has a visible short exhaust protruding outside the roof to release heat produced inside; the OV-SC has satellite antenna and rotating radar in its roof. The OV-SQ has no visible distinguishing feature relative to the OV-OE and OV-CC except that the OV-SQ is longer and has more doors on both sides. Wherever the operation is located, these vehicles do not park close to each other as much as possible except the OV-SQ and the OV-OE. The OV-SC and the OV-PG always situate themselves far from the rest of the vehicles but are able to spot any intruders through their radar and electronic surveillance systems."

Dexter's answer was very useful. Nathan appeared satisfied with it.

"You said earlier that your operation extracts all the organs from a source, which means killing the person." Nikandro wanted to confirm. "Is that correct?"

Dexter nods. "Yes, all organ sources subjected to extraction, unfortunately, have to die since most of the vital organs are gone. We do not have life sustaining support system to replace the organs that are removed. It is not part of the operational and business design."

Both Nathan and Nikandro could hardly believe what they heard. Nikandro asked in angry shaking voice, "And what do you do with the dead bodies?"

"They are placed in a plasma arc waste destruction system that transforms the dead bodies into their molecular elements without emission (Appendix C). Thus, the remains of organ sources are untraceable," replied

Dexter. The high electrical power required by the plasma gasification is supplied by a large Bloom Energy Server (Appendix D) that is used in tandem with the plasma gasification unit and also carried in the OV-PG. The BES produces power using solid fuel oxide cell technology without any harmful emissions. All OVs have their own onboard BES of varying sizes depending on the need.

"Our Chief of Police Joshua Dean was abducted and taken by one of your OVs yesterday. Why was he kidnapped," Nathan asked.

Dexter replied, "Chief Dean was never targeted as an organ source. We do not want to mess with him. He was just in the wrong place at the wrong time. But now he has become an organ source. There is no way he will be set free."

Nikandro's question was more forceful. "Can you lead us or at least point out where they brought him?"

"No, I can not. I do not know where they are camped now. All communication with them in our van has been disabled and they now consider our van an adversary vehicle." Dexter sounded apologetic with his reply.

Nathan persisted on the same line of questioning as Nikandro. "Where were they when you last delivered organ sources to them?"

"The OV-SQ was here in Camanor," Dexter replied. "We planned for it to be here all day yesterday until we completed our goal of having 16 organ sources. But our operation was interrupted by Police Chief Dean," Dexter explained.

"You said earlier that foreign doctors are brought from other countries since no American doctors want to work with your operation illegally extracting organs from unwilling persons, is that right?" asked Nathan.

"Yes, that's right," Dexter replied.

"When do you expect the foreign doctors to arrive, if they are not here yet and when are they scheduled to start organ extraction?" Nathan is more vigorous and direct in his question.

Dexter hesitated and looked up before answering. "Two doctors will arrive at the camp early tomorrow morning and will start organ extraction toward noon after they inspect the facilities and approve the preparation."

"I have no more questions for this guy." Nathan told Nikandro.

"So do I," Nikandro said. "Are we going to interrogate the other fellow?" Nikandro asked Nathan.

"I am satisfied with our information from Dexter. No need to question the other guy. We must conserve time." Nathan told Nikandro.

Dexter was shocked upon hearing this. He thought all along that the freshly cut tongue in the basin and the splattered fresh blood in the area were from his companion. Now he is regretfully realizing he has been tricked. His fear of reprisal from his boss for spilling the beans, so to speak, and the justice system he has to face in the future made him perspire profusely. He turned pale.

Nathan asked the two police officers to bring the suspects to the police headquarters. They are also carrying the original copy of the interrogation video to be handed over to Deputy Sturgess.

The two police officers were curious to know if they needed to accompany Nathan in rescuing Joshua. Nathan told them he would prefer to do it alone since we still have no idea where they are holding him. It will be complicated if they have to cross state lines. Nathan thanked them for their concern and offer to help. He assured them he will be communicating with Deputy Sturgess.

Although still not convinced about Nathan's safety and success in carrying out the rescue mission alone, the two police officers can not insist on accompanying him since Nathan had made his position clear. Of course, the police officers were not privy to the power of the Super Ring that Nathan carries along in his mission to rescue Joshua and the other kidnapped victims.

SABANG TRIBE WEAPONRY 10

*A*fter the interrogation, Nathan collected his thoughts and tried to communicate telepathically with Joshua. Suddenly he heard an unmistakable voice. "Father, I'm hearing you," Nathan blurted out. "Nikandro and I just completed questioning the leader of the two kidnappers who were in the tinted white van that I captured this morning after they kidnapped two Sabang teenagers. Their operation involves extracting all organs from their kidnapped victims and selling them in the domestic and international black market. Tomorrow two foreign doctors will arrive and extract organs from those they have kidnapped including yourself. I will not let that happen Father. I am going to rescue you and everyone." Nathan assured Joshua.

"Thank you, my Son. Hurry, but be careful." Joshua relayed to Nathan's mind the clear words of hope and concern. At this point emotions swelled between the two breaking the concentration and telepathic connection.

Nikandro knew Nathan was in contact with Joshua, so he did not interrupt. "Now that you're done talking with Joshua, I want to show you some ancient Sabang weaponry, which you may be able to use in your mission. Come." Nikandro led Nathan to an old wooden unpolished cabinet and opened it.

Among the items inside a wooden box are rough-rounded metal objects slightly smaller than a baseball. Nikandro picked one piece and showed it to Nathan saying, "This is a multiple exploding hand grenade. On impact, it will explode with devastating force. Two mini bombs inside will scatter during the first explosion with each small bomb creating a secondary explosion upon hitting hard objects. Thus the damage is multiplied several times. Unlike ordinary hand grenades, it does not have a pin and will explode only when it hits a hard object. In using this weapon accuracy in throwing is important, which of course is not a problem with you because of your skill as a football quarterback. The strength of the throw is also important but again not an issue with you because of your Super Ring strength."

Nikandro did not elaborate on the mechanism inside the bomb and Nathan did not ask.

Nikandro pulled out another wooden box. It contains star-shaped metal objects with sharp edges about five inches in circular diameter and one-half inch thick at the center. He told Nathan. "This is for silent killing of enemies. It is directed to any part of the body particularly the heart or neck of your human target. It is forcefully thrown like a frisbee. Unlike a boomerang it will not return to the thrower. A dried deadly mixture of poisonous materials including cobra venom, box jellyfish sting, scorpion venom and various plant extracts are laced at a point about one-half inch from the tips of the star weapon. The poison is released when a person is hit and the tip of the sharp end penetrates the skin by at least an inch. The poison is then absorbed by the blood and circulated to the brain and heart. Death is almost instantaneous and the person is unable to make any noise," Nikandro said.

"This is a lethal weapon," Nathan noted. "Based on what Officer Demos told me, this will come in handy against those people. I will really need it together with the multiple explosion bomb."

"I agree," Nikandro quickly replied. "Bring plenty of them." Nikandro added, "Always remember, however, that the best weapon you have is the power the Super Ring gave you. Use it to the full extent toward accomplishing your mission. While you have those powers, never forget that you are still a normal human being. You can be hurt, wounded, exhausted or sick and even die from any of the usual causes. You are still vulnerable to any physical and emotional harm that the enemies would inflict on you. Therefore, you have to be always conscious about the danger and be careful of yourself."

Nathan nodded without saying anything. Nikandro understood and was pleased with Nathan's response.

PERFECT MATCH 11

At Camanor High School, the news about Boyd and Lauren's kidnapping and the immediate, single-handed rescue by Nathan Dean has spread like wildfire. This came about since it was reported in the local media based on the information released by Police Deputy Chief Sturgess. The purpose of disseminating the information promptly was to alert the public of the presence in the locality of the kidnappers and to be vigilant all the time. However, for security reasons the face of Nathan was never shown in the report.

With Lauren's kidnapping her popularity soared, not because of anything she did or did not do. It was simply because Nathan was the "Knight of shining armor" who saved her much like the stuff of fairy tales. People talked about how perfect a match the two would make.

Nathan's awesome strength and speed during the rescue did not escape Lauren's notice despite being hooded. She was feeling all of it, from the sudden hard stop of the van to the whizzing sound of the wind generated by the speed of Nathan's movement. This created a dilemma for Lauren as she found herself thinking more and more of Nathan.

Lauren knew of Police Chief Dean's abduction. She was also aware that Nathan will try to rescue his father alone. Not knowing who the enemy was and what had happened to Joshua could happen to Nathan as well worried her. But her optimism kept her thinking – good always triumphs over evil.

Lauren veered her thoughts to Joshua's family. Although she has not met Nathan's family, she felt the anguish they must be experiencing. Lauren thought it would be best to drop by their home to thank them for her rescue and to boost their morale at this difficult time.

When cheer leading practice was over, Lauren decided to pass by the police headquarters first to inquire about the latest on the two kidnappers interrogated by Nikandro and Nathan. She also wanted to get the contact phone and address of Joshua's family.

As Lauren approaches the headquarters, she saw the two kidnappers being led by the two police officers, who accompanied Nathan to Nikandro's place. The suspects will be held temporarily in the headquarters for processing. With heads bowed low, both suspects seemed not to recognize nor even care about Lauren. To the suspects, Lauren could just be anyone of those people they have scrutinized as potential organ source. And Lauren felt she could have been in dire situation had Nathan not rescued her. This is what she surmised to be the current predicament of abducted Police Chief Dean. Unaware of the Super Ring, she hoped that Nathan's inherent skills and intelligence would be up to the challenge posed by the enemy.

Police Deputy Sturgess invited Lauren inside his room upon seeing her through the glass door talking to the clerk at the counter. Once Lauren is seated, Deputy Sturgess informed her. "Nathan's and Nikandro's interrogation of the suspects was successfully completed with the leader of the two revealing what they needed to know. I just sent Joshua's FBI friend, Special Agent William Stern at the Bureau's Washington head office, a copy of the interrogation video," the Deputy continued. "It's bewildering how these criminals can do such a thing! The Sabang people have to be really vigilant and careful." Deputy Sturgess' voice is full of anger as he shared the crux of the interrogation to Lauren.

"Where is Nathan now?" Lauren can not help herself from asking.

"He must have left Camanor about an hour ago to search for and rescue Joshua and the rest of the kidnapped Sabang victims," replied Deputy Sturgess.

"Is he alone?" Lauren inquired. "May be it would have been safer if some police officers accompanied him?" She opined hardly able to mask her concern.

"He asked to be alone for good reasons," Deputy Sturgess replied. "First, nobody knows where the kidnappers and their victims including Chief Dean are. They could be in another state, which really will get complicated if Camanor police officers are with Nathan. Also in this situation where very little is known of the enemy, numbers can work either way. But Nathan is in constant contact with us and the office of FBI Special Agent Stern in Washington, D.C." Deputy Sturgess tried to allay Lauren's fear for Nathan's safety.

"I hope everything turns out well," Lauren said. "As I often say, good always triumphs over evil."

"I hope so too, replied Deputy Sturgess. "Peace is what Camanor deserves and Joshua is irreplaceable to us."

Lauren bid Deputy Sturgess goodbye which he acknowledged gladly. "Good bye and be safe."

Lauren left the police headquarters.

Inside her car she phoned Mayfair. "Good afternoon, Mrs. Dean. My name is Lauren, Lauren Lark. I am one of the two Camanor High School students rescued by your son Nathan this morning. I would like to drop by your place, if you won't mind, at a convenient time for you. I would like to meet and personally thank you for what Nathan did to me."

"You are most welcome, Lauren. Anytime is fine. My daughter Eriga and myself will be pleased to have you visit us. How about dinner tonight, say 6:00?" Mayfair asked.

"That will be great," Lauren replied quite thrilled. Can I bring anything, dessert or something?" Lauren wanted to know.

"There's really no need, Lauren. But if it pleases you go ahead and whatever you bring will be greatly appreciated." Mayfair finds it hard to refuse Lauren's offer. Do you have our home address?" Mayfair wanted to make sure Lauren will not get lost on her way.

"Yes, Mrs. Dean." Deputy Sturgess at the Police headquarters was kind enough to give me the address and direction to your place." Lauren assured Mayfair.

"See you then at six, Lauren. Good bye." Mayfair will need additional items to prepare for dinner aside from what she had earlier intended for her and Eriga. She then phoned Eriga that she will be 10-15 minutes late in fetching her since she was passing by the grocery store for some items. Eriga was pleased to know that Lauren was coming for dinner.

Three minutes before six o'clock the door bell rang. Although Mayfair is certain it is Lauren, for security reason she checked first through the door's peep hole before disarming the home alarm system and opening the door. "Come in Lauren. We are happy you came." Mayfair greeted Lauren at the door.

"Good evening, Mrs. Dean." Lauren responded courteously. "I am glad it was easy finding your address and it was a fun drive all the way."

Eriga rushed to the living room from the kitchen to greet Lauren. "Hello Lauren! I am Eriga, Nathan's younger sister. You are really beautiful as they say you are," added Eriga before inviting Lauren to have a seat.

"Thank you for the compliment, Eriga. You yourself are beautiful," replied Lauren. She then told Mayfair that she brought a pecan pie, which she hopes they will like.

Mayfair took the pie that Lauren brought. "You should not have bothered. But it is well appreciated. We will have it for dessert." Mayfair then asked Eriga to talk to Lauren and make her feel at home while she prepares dinner.

"Can I help?" Lauren offered.

"Thank you, but only a few things are left to do. Dinner should be ready in a short while," Mayfair said.

The dining table is square and comfortably sits four persons. However, it is expandable to six. Mayfair sat on one side facing the kitchen. Lauren and Eriga were at opposite sides flanking Mayfair. Eriga offered the dinner prayer. Dinner is modest but healthy with baked chicken and fried tilapia for the main entree, dinner roll, lettuce salad, blanched baby carrots and broccoli for vegetables and fruits included pineapple, apples and grapes. Dessert, of course, is Lauren's pecan pie. Choice of coffee or tea was served with dessert. The dinner conversation was animated. Lauren and Eriga recalled funny school and sports experiences. Mayfair interjects what it was like during her days. Dinner ended with a prayer and wish for the successful rescue of Joshua and the rest of the Sabang kidnapped victims as well as Nathan's safe return. Lauren stayed chatting joyfully with Mayfair and Eriga for another hour after dinner. The three helped each other clean up the table.

Lauren left the Dean's household happy for having known Mayfair and Eriga better and with the thought that somehow she helped them boost their morale. As she was driving home, however, it was the image of Nathan that filled her mind. This is not a distraction for her though but a positive stimulus to drive carefully and safely.

TELEPATHIC COMMUNICATION 12

*A*fter Nikandro extensively briefed Nathan on the weaponry and various psychological and physical tactics, Nathan was ready to embark on his mission. He entered the white tinted van that was confiscated from the kidnappers. He and Nikandro decided it will be better to use the van to locate the enemies, who were expected to immediately attack it as it has become a hostile vehicle. Nathan sat quietly on the driver's seat, closing his eyes to concentrate and to telepathically connect with his father. Almost immediately, he said, "Father, I am now leaving Camanor to look for you. I will be guided by Eagle Spirit in my search. Please call him now so that he can zero in on your location. Is there anything you can tell me about where you might be?" Nathan asked.

"There is, my Son," Nathan heard Joshua through his mind. "Since my timepiece was confiscated, I just counted the number of seconds based on my heartbeat, to figure out the travel time to our destination or what could be their current base of operation. All together we traveled for about 27,000 seconds equivalent to seven and a half hours. For about 16,200 seconds or 4.5 hours of that we were traveling fast on what felt like an interstate freeway because there were lots of traffic. I could hear 18-wheeler cargo trucks as I reckoned from their engine noise. We then exited to a state highway and traveled for about 9,000 seconds or about 2.5 hours there. The RV then made a sharp right turn into a paved road and traveled for 1800 seconds or half an hour at very slow speed of may be 30 miles per hour. With an average speed of 70 mph, travel time of 4.5 hours could have covered 315 miles. Similarly, the 9,000 seconds or 2.5 hours of travel at a slower speed of 60 mph could have covered 150 miles and 30 mph for half an hour, about 15 miles. So, we are about 480 miles north of Camanor. I figured north since the giant RV that abducted me was facing north then and I did not feel a sharp turn from that position until we were near the destination."

"Father, this is vital information for me and Eagle Spirit." Nathan told Joshua. "Eagle Spirit can now fly at some altitude and get a fix on your possible location, much like a GPS. Once done, he can then fly at lower altitude making it easier for me to follow him especially on major turns."

There was sudden noise from a passing military helicopter that interrupted Nathan's concentration and communication with Joshua. But he was happy with the information he got from his father.

Nathan mentally informed Eagle Spirit about the approximate distance of Joshua's northward location. Eagle Spirit quickly climbed to an altitude Nathan could only guess to be about 25,000 feet. He then circled around an area several times for nearly two minutes at a location Nathan would not know how far. Eagle Spirit then dived back and perched on a big tree at Nikandro's compound where Nathan was with the van. At this tree, Eagle Spirit waited for instruction.

"We should be going, Eagle Spirit." Nathan telepathically told Eagle Spirit, who responded by flapping his wings. "But before we go, let me contact Father for one last thing he might tell me." Nathan concentrated as if in deep thought. Joshua immediately responded as he was himself waiting for Nathan to get in touch.

"Nathan, I want you to give to FBI Special Agent Stern through Deputy Sturgess my approximate location of 480 miles north of Camanor. If at all possible, Agent Stern should try to be in Camanor tonight to be closer to my location once you get a fix on it. He should know I am okay so far. But time is of the essence," Joshua instructed.

"I'll do that right away, Father." Nathan answered and immediately relayed Joshua's message for FBI Agent Stern to Deputy Sturgess.

Agent Stern is like a brother to Joshua. They trained together with the Navy Seal and fought along side in the Iran conflict, the last regional war America got involved in after clearing itself out of the Iraq and Afghanistan wars. They were both awarded the Purple Heart for bravery in action especially for repulsing the attack by hundreds of enemy fighters on a downed rescue helicopter evacuating dozens of wounded US soldiers.

Once on their way, Eagle Spirit flew at about 250 feet above where Nathan could easily see him. Nathan is aware that because he was driving he could not focus his sight on Eagle Spirit for long periods as he needed to keep an eye on the road to prevent accidents. For straight sections of the freeway this was not a problem. However, when the road curved even a little, Nathan made sure his eyes were on the road. Eagle Spirit impressed Nathan with the way he guided him. In long stretches, Eagle Spirit flew well ahead of him along side the road. Sometimes he disappeared in the horizon for several minutes and then reappeared. At intersections or exits, Eagle Spirit would circle around several times. As Nathan's van neared him, Eagle Spirit would fly toward the direction they were going, making sure Nathan saw the intersection or exit they were taking. Then Eagle Spirit would continue his flight with Nathan on the tail.

Nathan observed that several motorists were looking at the eagle flying over the highway. They appeared curious about a stray eagle with shiny well-groomed feathers. So far this did not cause any traffic problem or any disturbance to delay Nathan.

After traveling for just a little over four hours, Nathan noticed he was running low on fuel. It was also getting dark at about 8:00 o'clock in the evening. Sunset was usually late as summer was approaching. Although Nathan estimated he could still cover another 40 miles with the gasoline left in his tank, he thought that for his sake and also for Eagle Spirit he should pull over the next gasoline station along the way to gas up and stretch his limbs a little bit. He wanted to ensure that he had enough fuel as he nears the camp of the organ syndicate holding Joshua and the other Sabang kidnapped victims.

MR. 'ROBIN HOOD' 13

*N*athan saw a billboard indicating gas, food, lodging in the next exit from the interstate. He exited and decided to stop at the gasoline station for some gas after communicating with Eagle Spirit. Nathan noticed that only one car was parked near the store's door with one person, a young man in his twenties, seated on the driver's side. Another car just drove away without loading gasoline. Nathan was curious, but pulled in along side one pump anyway.

When he inserted his credit card on the payment machine at the pump, however, it was rejected. He now had to go to the cashier inside the store. He was on his way inside when the young man stepped out of the parked car and prevented him from going inside.

Irritated, Nathan told the young man. "I just want to pay for gasoline. I don't see anything wrong with that."

"It is all wrong because I said you can not go inside so you can not. Besides I had the door locked," the young man replied. The young man then pulled a gun and was going to pistol whip Nathan in the head. Nathan caught his arm holding the gun in mid-air and twisted it slowly until the young man cried in pain. He dropped the gun on the concrete floor. Nathan gave the young man a chop at the back of his neck rendering him unconscious.

Nathan then picked up the gun and bent its barrel. He grabbed some handcuffs from his van and handcuffed the still unconscious young man to the steering wheel of the car. He also twisted the car key so it can not be used anymore to start the vehicle.

When Nathan looked closer inside the store through the glass door, he saw a robbery in progress. There were two young holduppers inside both with automatic pistols. An elderly person, presumably the owner of the store, was held by one of the young holdupper in the inner section of the store with the gun pressed on his temple. The other holdupper, also a young man was watching an elderly lady, presumably the wife of the owner, transfer money to a leather bag from the cash register situated close to the door. Nathan realized then that the car outside was a getaway car and the young man that stopped him from getting inside was the driver of the three-man holdup gang.

After some thought, Nathan barged inside the store through the locked door. With the element of surprise, Nathan was able to immediately disarm the young holdupper in front of the cash register with the elderly lady and knocked him unconscious with his now trademark karate chop at the back of the neck. Nathan handcuffed the unconscious young man, took the gun and bent the barrel the same way he did with the other gun. The holduppers inside the store did not know what happened outside so they were surprised to see Nathan.

"Stop there or I will kill him," the young holdupper holding the elderly man shouted at Nathan pressing the gun on the man's temple harder and moving slightly backward away from Nathan.

"Relax guys." Nathan tried to calm the holdupper. "I will not harm you. Just release the old man and you will get all you want from here, money, soda and more, and you will be well on your way. He is innocent and has not done you any harm. He's just trying to earn a living while serving us motorists." Nathan inched slowly toward the stock of soda drinks located on the side where the young holdupper was holding the owner of the store.

"Stop, I said." The young man yelled and is getting visibly annoyed. "Innocent or not I will kill him if you continue moving toward me."

"I have an older brother your age," Nathan said. Although not true, he was trying to psychologically manipulate the young holdupper. "He made a wrong choice like you that he lived to regret for 20 years in prison – kill an innocent person. Come on, let the old man go."

"I have been to prison before and I hate it like anything." The young holdupper said calmly. "They do not reform you there. They just punish you. And when you get out after paying your debt, society frowns on you. Getting an honest job is next to impossible. We are then forced to do this dirty thing again and again and again. The cycle of hell just continues."

The young holdupper is starting to touch Nathan's sense of humanity and compassion. So too was the old man he was holding at gun point.

"Like now we do not want to do this." The young man said. "We have nothing to eat or a decent place to stay for the night. We sleep in the car wherever we can park overnight. We have not had lunch and do not know where dinner will come from. With my jail record, no one dares to employ me. They are afraid of ex-convicts."

"What's your name, by the way." Nathan asked in a brotherly tone.

"Shawn Brown." The young holdupper replied humbly.

Nathan detected that Shawn has now loosened his hold on the old man and has moved the barrel of the gun away from his temple. The old man was now breathing easier and looked more relaxed.

"But you will change your ways if someone gives you a chance to do decent work?" Nathan asked while searching the old man for a reaction.

"Of course I will. I have wanted to do that long time ago. I lack education but I am willing to do any honest manual work. Unlike me who do not have a family, my two friends here belong to wealthy families, who can give them both love and a decent living. But they chose to join me for the sake of friendship. If I am not in this predicament they will be much better off because then their families will not renounce them for going around with an ex-convict." The young man was emotional and clearly feeling sorry for himself.

"May I speak?" The old man, not anymore held by Shawn, asked. Then he said, "My name is Richard Lim.

I have owned this store for more than 20 years now. My wife has long been wanting to retire but could not because nobody is around to help me. Our children are all professionals and have better jobs elsewhere." He paused, took a deep breath and continued. "If Shawn promises me, my wife and especially Mr. Robin Hood here, pointing to Nathan, that he will be a reformed and good person and will work hard for an honest living, I am offering him a full-time job starting tomorrow to assist me in the store."

Shawn could not believe what he heard. "Am I dreaming?" He asked himself. There is a moment of silence from everyone. When Shawn realized that a decent and honest job offer was just made by the very person he was ready to kill, tears flowed from his eyes. He embraced Richard and thanked him like no other. "I promise, I promise you, your wife and Mr. Robin Hood that I will be a good person and will work hard for an honest living." Richard, his wife and Nathan were all euphoric.

"By the way, my name is Nathan Dean." Nathan told everybody. "I am not Robin Hood. I have an urgent mission far from here so I can not stay long. But I will visit this place again later to see how Shawn is doing on his promise for a new life."

Richard faces Nathan saying, "Whatever your name is, to me you always will be the legendary Robin Hood for what you did and how you did it. Let me help with the gas outside. A full tank is on the house."

At this time Shawn's friend inside the store who was earlier unconscious woke up. He seemed to understand what had happened and he too was happy for Shawn.

Outside the store, the guy handcuffed in the steering wheel also regained consciousness now and was trying to extricate himself. Nathan approached and told him everything was all right now and removed the handcuff. The guy was perplexed about it until Shawn, who followed Nathan and Richard outside to help, explained.

After putting a full tank of premium gasoline and repairing the car key, Nathan turned to Richard and said, "Good bye, Richard. You were right in giving Shawn a chance to change his life which society failed to do. You and your family as well as your business will be blessed." He then turned to Shawn and told him. "I know you will not fail yourself and all of us witnesses to today's event. You too will be blessed." He then drove away certain that Eagle Spirit was with him.

Nathan was happy for what he had done - - saved the life of Richard and changed for good the lives of Shawn and his two friends. Although it was not part of his mission, it gave him a sense of accomplishment nonetheless.

LOCATING THE ENEMY BASE 14

*F*rom Richard's gasoline station and before reaching the interstate, Nathan saw the motel advertised in the billboard he passed by earlier. He thought it was getting dark and after a very long day it was time to turn in. He freshened up, had a good dinner, slept as much as he could and headed to his mission at daybreak. Eagle Spirit, meanwhile, settled on a big tree at the back of the motel.

Before going to bed, Nathan checked his cell phone for messages. Deputy Sturgess told Nathan that per his message, FBI Special Agent Stern left Washington, D.C. together with four other agents in the afternoon after receiving Joshua's message and were expected to arrive in Camanor at about 2:00 o'clock the following morning. Mayfair informed Nathan about their dinner at home with Lauren, who she found quite charming. She said Lauren visited to thank them and Nathan for rescuing her from the kidnappers and to boost their spirits during this challenging time. Nathan was at the moment unmoved. His mind was set on his mission and did not want another distraction like the Shawn Brown episode at Richard's gasoline station.

Nathan communicated to Joshua to inform him of Agent Stern's message. Joshua was glad. He knew he can always depend on his war buddy and friend William.

Nathan had a good six hours of sleep, awakened only by the wake-up call he requested from the hotel desk. At daybreak, which was about 5:00 A.M. Nathan was ready to take off. Sensing that Eagle Spirit is already waiting, Nathan moved on.

After about half an hour on the interstate, Nathan exited to a state highway. He thought this must be the road where the giant RV's speed was reduced from about 70 mph before in the interstate to only about 60 mph.

Nathan observed after one hour on the state highway that the landscape changed from industrial-urban to agricultural-rural.

Nathan wanted to get from Joshua some indicators that he was on the right track. He pulled over to the side of the road and flashed the van's emergency lights.

He then focused his thoughts until Joshua responded. "Father, if we are on the right direction, we should be where you are being held in about two hours." Nathan told Joshua. "We are passing an agricultural area with mixed crops, vegetables, grains and orchards with patches of cattle farms. Would you have any sense if the giant RV passed through this place?" inquired Nathan.

There was a momentary pause, then Joshua replied. "I remember that the air coming out of the RV air conditioner was a little heavier then it became fresher as we traveled along. When the RV reached its destination, cracking sounds of big doors opening could be heard and the RV maneuvered to park inside what felt like a large structure. It could be an empty hangar, a warehouse or vacant factory." Joshua was giving Nathan anything and everything he could recall.

To Nathan, these were helpful in convincing him that he was on the right track. "Thank you, Father, I believe we are on the right road. I can see from afar that Eagle Spirit is constantly circling a point further out in the direction of our travel."

"Be careful, Son." Joshua said, always mindful of Nathan's safety.

Aware that the vehicle he was driving has been tagged by the organ syndicate as an adversary, Nathan took special precaution along the way. He did not want to be surprised by a sneak attack either from the air or from land particularly from behind. While focusing on the road, he was keenly aware of his surroundings and regularly checked the rear view mirror for any vehicle behind him.

Before reaching the area where Joshua felt the RV made a full right turn, Nathan saw on the right side of the road a big sign saying "TriStar Products: Fruit and Vegetable Processing Facility 15 miles" with an arrow pointing to the right. The sign board appeared unkempt. It was also vandalized with a red letter X painted across the entire board. Nathan surmised that the place must have been vacated or abandoned for a while.

When Nathan saw Eagle Spirit circle an area less than one mile ahead, he said to himself. "This must be it, finally!" He took a deep breath and resumed his cautious driving.

Then the full 90-degree right turn came. A speed limit of 30 mph was posted on the side. "This must be the road Joshua remembered the RV making a full right turn and moving much slower before making the turn." Nathan murmured to himself.

Nathan's heart was beating faster in anticipation of what lies ahead. He touched the Super Ring with his left hand and gave it a circular motion as if to let it breathe and refresh its position in the middle finger of his right hand that is now holding the steering wheel.

Nathan knew the power of the Super Ring in his finger. He also kept in mind what Nikandro told him to always remember that he is still a normal human being that could be hurt, wounded, fatigued and even die from any of the usual causes. He is not immune to any physical and emotional harm the enemies would inflict. Against this background is his limited information about the enemies except their ruthlessness as assessed by Officer Demos and from what was revealed by Dexter during interrogation.

As he moved forward, Nathan's thoughts seesawed between sending the fix on Joshua's possible position to Deputy Sturgess now or wait a little while until he actually sees the OV and risk an attack by the syndicate. If he waited too long, precious time is lost for Special Agent Stern to come to their aid. On the other hand, sending the wrong location, will jeopardize the mission as they have to start all over again with the search. Special Agent Stern would have wasted his efforts.

Nathan's contemplation was cut short. When the van was about one mile from supposed destination, Nathan saw what appeared to be a helicopter drone moving fast from the opposite direction.

DRONE ATTACK 15

*N*arrowing his eyesight on the approaching helicopter drone, Nathan noticed a miniaturized air-to-ground missile on its belly and two machine guns on both sides of the body. The missile was released targeting the van. A turret of machine gun fire soon followed. Nathan quickly swerved the van to the left. The missile missed the van but the machine gun hit its right side damaging both right front and rear tires. The van was completely disabled. A siren alerting the presence of intruders sounded. Nathan could hear it from where the van was attacked.

Mustering all the speed power from the Super Ring, Nathan picked up the leather bag containing all the weapons and other deadly gadgets that Nikandro gave him. His communication and GPS equipment were already in his pocket. He jumped out of the van and raced toward a grove of big trees around the facility. The drone lost sight of him.

Nathan then noticed one OV parked outside a building with rotating radar at the roof. He immediately relayed to Deputy Sturgess the GPS fix on the facility and added he was under attack. Clearly, this was the current base of operation of the organ syndicate.

After a few seconds, the drone found Nathan again and fired both machine guns on him. Quickly using the big tree to shield him, Nathan was spared. He then sprinted toward another tree while the drone was searching for him. When the drone saw him, Nathan fortunately was able to take cover in another tree before the machine guns fired. The big trees around the facility were making it difficult for the drone to take aim at Nathan, whose unearthly agility was no match for the drone.

Nathan took out one of Nikando's multiple-explosion bombs. As the drone made a pass close to the tree shielding him, he hurled the bomb toward it blasting it to smithereens.

The OV-SC then released a sub-compact radio-controlled armored fighting vehicle (AFV). Nathan could hear the sound of its wheels on the dry grass around the facility. Nathan is fully aware of its approach. When it appeared in full view, Nathan tossed a multiple-explosion bomb toward it before the AFV could fire a machine gun mounted on its top. It was a hit and there was a loud explosion. However, the AFV was not even dented and continued to charge toward Nathan. The bomb did not penetrate its thick metal shell. It fired at Nathan using the machine gun on its top and the two other guns mounted on each side above the wheels. Only Nathan's quick movement out of the line of fire saved him. Since Nathan was now on the left side of the AFV after evading its frontal attack, he placed a bomb in front of its left wheel. The AFV ran over the bomb which exploded, but did no damage.

As he kept running from cover to cover to avoid the blazing gunfire from the AFV, Nathan saw a pond that used to have water fountains. The fountain nozzles were still there and were visible as the pond was almost empty except for a foot or so deep of water that has turned green due to thick algae. The pond is about three feet deep with vertical concrete walls all around.

The AFV continued to chase Nathan raining gun fire on him without let up. Nathan observed that the gun on top of the AFV rotates a complete 360 degrees with a line of fire about two and a half feet above the ground. The two guns on the side, which were about 1.5 feet above ground both swang left to right at an angle of 90 degrees and also had vertical movement of 30 degrees above and 10 degrees below the horizontal.

With this in mind, Nathan knew that he can approach the AFV from the rear if he crawled lower than 2.5 feet or if the gun at the top was pointed in front. With blinding speed and marshaling all the strength from the Super Ring, Nathan then pushed the AFV toward the pond.

The AFV fell on the pond upside down. Resting on its top, the AFV could not do anything to correct its position. The shallow water in the pond was enough to cause a short circuiting of its battery-run electrical system. Thick smoke bellowed from the AFV.

BLACK HAWK HELICOPTER 16

*M*eanwhile back in Camanor, Special Agent Stern has plotted the GPS fix on the target area that Nathan sent through Police Deputy Sturgess. Agent Stern has also obtained a Google map of the location. The map indicates that the place has not been functional for sometime as shown by the overgrown weeds and shrubs surrounding the buildings. A concrete helicopter landing site is clearly seen on the map. Although the surface of the landing pad has plenty of light debris, Agent Stern was happy to see it. The near empty fountain pond where Nathan pushed the AFV can also be seen. Prominent on the map is a large warehouse aside from several other structures. From what Agent Stern could gather, activity in the facility ceased nearly five years ago due to unresolved dispute between labor and management, which was further complicated by the entry of outside agitators with their own agenda.

More interesting was what Agent Stern saw from the enhanced Google infrared satellite map. It showed fresh tire marks from heavy vehicles indicating recent traffic activity involving large equipment. There were few tire marks from smaller vehicles too. However, Agent Stern could only see two OVs. The rest of the OVs were not visible on the Google map. Although the unseen OVs puzzled Agent Stern, the available information confirmed the use of the facility by the organ syndicate. He surmised that the other OVs could be hidden inside the warehouse.

For this mission, Agent Stern uses the latest version of the battle-proven workhorse, Black Hawk helicopter. Its weight has been greatly reduced with the use of carbon fiber materials for its body and rotors thus greatly increasing its speed and payload capacity. It is fitted with the most sophisticated avionics and electronics now available in the industry. Most of all, it has battery-operated electric motor technology, which the automotive industry already began using in the early twenty first century. The aviation industry later adopted the technology in helicopters and light airplanes. Agent Stern's Black Hawk helicopter is already battery-operated and does not use jet fuel anymore. Thus, it is emission-free, a benefit to the environment. More importantly, it tremendously increased its speed and payload capacity. The Black Hawk carries four battery packs with each pack capable of five hours of flight. Maximum charge time for the batteries is two hours. The pilot has completed charging the battery that they used on the D.C. flight. The chopper has now four fresh power supply packs.

After a quick chat with the agent piloting the chopper, Agent Stern called it a go, assembled his team of four other agents and informed Deputy Sturgess of their departure from Camanor. At an average cruising speed of 300 mph, the pilot estimated that they will reach the target site in one hour and forty minutes. Agent Stern clearly did not want to be late for Joshua's rescue, not certain how well Nathan was holding up with his part of the mission.

In retrospect, Agent Stern wondered how Joshua was able to discern the distance where he was brought and how Nathan was able to get it from him and ultimately locate the precise mobile headquarters of the organ syndicate. He met Nathan as a young boy but not as a grown-up. While he could not say much about him, he knew that with Joshua anything is possible. If Nathan took on from his father, he had reason to be optimistic.

Of course Agent Stern knew nothing about the power of the Sabang ancestral spirits. Such power was difficult to explain, more so to comprehend. Outside of the Dean family, perhaps only Nikandro and Deputy Sturgess knew the extent of that power and how it is tapped.

Deputy Sturgess had a last-minute talk with Agent Stern regarding Nathan. When informed that Nathan had not communicated lately, Agent Stern began to worry. He told Deputy Sturgess, "I hope nothing bad had happened to Nathan and that we could still help him rescue his father."

Deputy Sturgess assured Agent Stern that he was confident Nathan was all right since he had not sent a distress signal. Encouraged, Agent Stern quickly boarded the Black Hawk helicopter and took off.

FIRE ANT MOUND 17

*A*fter knocking out the mini helicopter drone and the AFV, Nathan noticed he was not being pursued by armed personnel of the organ syndicate. Although puzzled, Nathan began entertaining the idea that the syndicate may actually have limited number of security personnel. If this was true, they might have shifted from an offensive to a defensive strategy after losing two of its fighting machines to Nathan. Recalling the video that Officer Demos was able to make when Chief Dean was abducted, Nathan was convinced that the syndicate could be relying more on the radio-controlled weaponry installed in its organ vehicles together with only a handful of armed personnel assigned in each OV. Nathan must keep this in mind especially that the OV-SC and the OV-PG are parked only about 150 feet from each other. Nathan still has to locate the three other OVs.

With striking speed, Nathan circled the OV-SC twice. He mainly was baiting the OV-SC to expose its RC machine guns or whatever weapons it had. The ruse worked as slowly five windows opened on the OV-SC, two on each side and one at the back of the vehicle. Machine gun turrets could be seen in each window and these were scanning for targets. No armed security showed up yet. However, Nathan now has a clear idea on how to destroy this OV-SC and flush out the people inside.

Again using his lightning speed and moving only five feet away from the OV-SC, Nathan threw one multiple-explosion bomb through each open window. A series of explosions erupted followed by detonating ammunition triggered by the fire inside that was generated by the bomb.

Four armed personnel scampered out of the OV-SC each with an assault rifle and fired indiscriminately. Nathan took cover beside a big tree and could not be seen from the OV-SC area. The pants of one armed personnel caught fire and he was frantically putting it out. Another security guard, who was slightly wounded on his right leg must have seen part of Nathan's clothes and started firing toward the tree. When he paused to reload the rifle with new magazine, Nathan threw a star weapon at him hitting him in the neck. The man died almost instantly. And because he was unable to make any sound his other companions did not know he was already killed.

Nathan then rapidly moved to another tree some 60 feet away. The two armed men continued pumping bullets on Nathan's previous location. They were joined by the man with the burned pants after he extinguished the flame. Because of the speed with which Nathan was moving, they did not see that he has shifted locations. More bullets pelted the tree that Nathan first occupied. The three men jointly inspected the tree they pumped a lot of bullets on hoping to find a dead or wounded person. They found nothing.

After briefly talking on how to flush out the intruder, the three men spread themselves 100 feet apart in a flanking formation and walked toward the line of big trees. The tree where Nathan had taken cover was right on their path and sandwitched between the man at the center and the man to the right. When the men were about 30 feet away from the tree, Nathan made a quick dash in the opposite direction and between the man at the center and the man to the right. Caught by surprise, the two men furiously opened fire toward the fast moving target they could only guessed as a person. By firing in opposite directions, they actually ended up hitting and killing each other. Nathan also had a bullet scrape his left arm. While putting a tourniquet to stop the bleeding, Nathan said to himself. "My strategy worked as two men were killed by their own bullets, but it was too risky to repeat. I won't do it again."

The third man rushed to his two companions on the ground. Upon seeing them both dead, he raged and fired his rifle aimlessly. When it was time to reload, Nathan hit him in the stomach with a star weapon. He died instantly.

The indiscriminate firing by the third man hit twice the OV-PG parked close by. This triggered an unintended opening of its three weapon windows - one on each side and one at the back. When Nathan saw the machine gun turrets scanning for targets, he instantly grabbed three multiple-explosion bombs and threw one in each weapon window. Deafening explosions reverberated in the otherwise tranquil area.

Three bloodied individuals emerged from the OV-PG that carried its plasma gasification unit and the large Bloom Energy Server, which was still exploding inside. One of the men could barely stand. With his leg wound bleeding profusely, he had to sit down on the concrete pavement with rifle cocked ready to kill. The two other men, one of whom was slightly limping due to shrapnel wound on his thigh, started scouring around hoping to find the intruder. When they did not see anyone since Nathan was hiding on the other side of the vehicle, they joined the other man sitting on the pavement.

Nathan overheard one man said, "Two of our companions died from the blast. I tried pulling them out of the rubble but gave up because they were already dead."

The other man uttered, "We must find and kill this intruder or we and the entire operation are history."

Nathan could only smile as evidently these men were unaware that the OV-SC has been completely damaged. Now even their OV-PG is exploding. But this was not enough for Nathan since he had not located Joshua and the other kidnapped victims. He now must find the vehicle holding them.

Using his super human speed, Nathan surprised the three armed guards by grabbing their rifles and hitting them in the head with the butt. They were all rendered unconscious. Nathan handcuffed and tied all of them together in a hydrant near where the OV-PG was parked.

While waiting for the three men to regain consciousness, Nathan hurriedly looked inside the OV-PG. He was curious if it had been recently used. He was glad to note that there was no sign of activity for the past day. Before exiting the still burning vehicle, Nathan disabled the connection between the BES and the plasma gasification unit not earlier destroyed by the multiple-explosion bombs.

At the hydrant, the three men regained consciousness and were trying to extricate themselves. Sheer disbelief filled their faces when they saw the boyish 17-year old intruder. They were wondering how this young intruder could single-handedly derail their operation despite its high-tech weaponry, sophisticated surveillance system and seasoned security personnel. Of course, they had no idea of the supernatural power of the Super Ring, which High Cloud gave to Nathan for the rescue of Joshua and the dismantling of the organ syndicate.

"Gentlemen," Nathan said in a calm calculated voice. "I want to have a frank conversation with you. Who will be your spokesperson?"

"He will." The two men pointed to the guy who could hardly stand due to his leg wound.

"What's your name?" Nathan asked the man.

"Is that important?" replied the man in a challenging manner.

Nathan retorted. "Why, is your name not important?" What then do they call you? Or how do you want me to call you? Darth Vader? Mickey Mouse? or what?"

"My name is Lambert; you can call me that." The man answered in a more civil tone.

"Thank you, Lambert." Nathan reciprocated the civility. "We can now talk more intelligently." Nathan is treading carefully for fear of Lambert suddenly withdrawing from the conversation. Nathan continued, "Your operation has a total of five organ vehicles. These two vehicles you call OV-SC and OV-PG are already disabled. Where could the other three be?

Lambert hesitated to tell the truth until prodded by the limping man who happened to be on top of a fire ant mound beside the hydrant. "You have to tell him what he wants. He must get us out of this hydrant. I can no longer endure these ants," said the limping man.

Nathan felt sorry about it. He did not intend to put anyone over a fire ant mound. It was there by chance. It was, however, a blessing in disguise because it would help him get a quick answer.

"They are all inside that big warehouse." Lambert told Nathan, pointing to the warehouse adjacent to where the OV-PG is parked.

"Are the doors locked?" Nathan asked.

Lambert said, "No, but it is opened only by an electric motor that is switched manually from inside. The person doing it gets in or out the warehouse through a small door on the left side. Since there are people in the warehouse, the small door is now locked from the inside."

Nathan then queried. "Where are the vehicles facing and are they all facing in one direction?

"All three vehicles are facing that main door." Lambert pointed to the front door of the warehouse.

"By the way," Nathan is again changing the topic. "The two foreign doctors, who will extract the organs, are they inside now? Have they arrived?"

"No, they were expected later this morning. But we lost contact with their helicopter when communication was disrupted and never restored with the destruction of the security and communication vehicle. We could not even tell them to divert destination because of the troubles you are causing us. They could be here in less than 30 minutes." Lambert now looking serious reiterated the request from the limping man. "Please move us out of this hydrant as the ants are feasting on us. They have spread and are now all over our body. They will kill us."

Nathan found the information that Lambert gave useful. He was ready to grant the request of the man on top of the fire ant mound. He found a smaller tree nearby and moved the three men there. He freed all their hands so that they can remove the ants from their body. The unscratched man tried to break away. But Nathan's mild karate chop on the back of his neck nearly cost him his consciousness. He then changed his mind and followed whatever Nathan said. The two other men both of whom had wounds simply did not have much choice.

Once Nathan got the three men securely tied under the tree, he picked up one of the assault rifles and rushed to the side of the warehouse where the small door mentioned by Lambert was. Nathan's priority now was to rescue Joshua and the rest of the kidnapped victims.

Nathan is conscious that Joshua and the other kidnapped victims should be rescued unharmed, if at all possible. He is also aware that at this point of his rescue effort, he is relying heavily on the information extracted from Lambert, who is a member of the syndicate – an enemy. Lambert did not voluntarily give the information but through the prodding of his companions, who together with him happened to be tied over a mound of fire ants. He must always keep this in mind to avoid surprises from the enemy such as security personnel waiting for him inside with drawn guns or being trapped inside the warehouse. In any case, he should avoid any risk that could jeopardize his rescue mission and that of Agent Stern.

RESCUING JOSHUA 18

*U*sing the rifle butt, Nathan forced open the small door of the warehouse. With only a thud, it was unnoticed by the men inside the organ vehicles.

Based on Dexter's information that he got during the interrogation at Nikandro's compound, Nathan immediately determined among the three OVs inside the warehouse which organ vehicle is holding Joshua and the other kidnapped victims. Having used all his remaining multiple-explosion bombs in destroying the OV-PG, Nathan must now employ another strategy for Joshua's rescue.

Nathan thought he should try to communicate telepathically with Joshua to inform him of his presence inside the warehouse and that he had identified the vehicle where they are being held. Although the condition is far from ideal for deep thought, Nathan decided it was worth trying.

Standing on one side of the vehicle with his right ear practically glued to the side in an effort to find out what was happening inside, Nathan said in his mind. "Father, I am outside the vehicle that is holding you. I will enter it at the right moment. Please let the guard walk you around."

Tense moments ensued. After a few seconds, Nathan was pleased to hear Joshua's voice. "Guard, guard, I badly need to go to the restroom. Please help me."

Nathan overheard a reply, "Wait a minute, I'm coming." It was the guard in charge of the kidnapped victims who also held the master key for all the handcuffs and shackles on the victims.

The guard came and got Joshua out from where he was restrained, which was to a 2-inch stainless pipe laid horizontally six inches above the floor. This allowed him to sit down on the floor and enabled him to have some lateral movement while seated. With handcuffs at his back, Joshua's feet were also shackled limiting his lateral motion. He walked slowly.

When Nathan was certain that the guard had accompanied Joshua to the restroom, he pried open one door of the OV-SQ and entered the vehicle. He signaled the surprised kidnapped victims through his lips to keep quite. He asked them where the guard brought Joshua.

Almost simultaneously, everyone pointed toward the front of the vehicle.

Nathan anxiously waited for Joshua and the guard to emerge from the restroom. He was holding a star weapon. When they came out, Joshua was in front with the guard at his back. The guard saw Nathan and immediately drew his handgun to shoot him. However, before the pistol could leave the holster, Nathan shouted. "Make way!" gesturing Joshua to duck, which he instantly did. Nathan hurled the star weapon, hitting the guard on the right shoulder. He dropped dead before he could fire his gun.

Quickly, Nathan took the master key from the fallen guard. He removed Joshua's handcuff and gave him the key to release his shackle.

The guard's fall on the floor made a loud thud, which was audible to the other men in the OV-SQ. "What's happening there? Are you all right, Windsor?" Someone asked. When there was no reply, another asked. "Windsor, Windsor, is there anything going on there?"

Joshua decided to answer. "He fainted. Windsor need immediate help!"

Two men rushed to look at what had happened to Windsor. Before they could reach the door, Joshua grabbed the guard's gun and as the men showed themselves Joshua fired two simultaneous shots hitting both of them between their eyes. They fell dead on the floor.

Joshua told Nathan while continuing to open his shackle. "Only one guy, the tranquilizer man is left. He is in the men's quarter where the other two came from." Nathan ran toward the man, who was surprised but immediately picked up a tranquilizer syringe. The man raised his arm holding the syringe to strike at Nathan. Catching his arm in the air, Nathan twisted it until the sounds of broken bones and excruciating cries filled the small room. The man dropped the tranquilizer syringe. Applying his trademark karate chop, the man dropped on the floor unconscious. Nathan lifted the man by his collar and face down pulled him toward Joshua, who was busy freeing the other kidnapped victims from their handcuffs and shackles. "Please take care of him, Father while I send urgent message to Deputy Sturgess." Nathan requested Joshua.

Joshua handcuffed and shackled the still-unconscious tranquilizer man and securely tied him to a 2-1/2 inch stainless steel vertical pipe at the center of the vehicle. He was restrained in such a manner that he could not sit down and had very limited lateral motion with his body and limbs.

Nathan's message to Deputy Sturgess, which was simultaneously received by Agent Stern in the Black Hawk helicopter, was brief as follows: "Joshua others rescued unharmed x chopper with foreign doctors ETA site 12 minutes but might divert or withdraw upon seeing destruction here x still in mopping ops."

Agent Stern immediately replied via Deputy Sturgess, "Copy, my ETA site 10 minutes."

All the kidnapped victims were now freed from their handcuffs and shackles. Joshua has already grabbed a rifle. Nathan approached Joshua and said to him. "Father, the giant RV beside this vehicle, which they call OV-OE, is where they extract the organs. The chopper carrying the foreign doctors, who were going to do the extraction were expected to land in 12 minutes. I informed Agent Stern accordingly and he has acknowledged. He is arriving here in about two minutes ahead of the organ chopper." Nathan then continued briefing Joshua. "The OV-OE has three radio-controlled machine guns installed at the rear and both sides of the vehicle. These guns show up when the window opens to scan for targets. The vehicle next to it on the other side is where the syndicate bosses and other medical staff stay. They call it OV-CC or the command center. It is a smaller RV and has radio-controlled machine gun at the rear. It also has several gun ports on two sides. At present, there are four people there. The director of this operation, who is meeting the foreign doctors at an airport, is with the doctors in the helicopter."

FATHER AND SON TEAM 19

*J*oshua told Nathan, "Okay Nathan, you take this vehicle beside us or the OV-OE and I will take the one at the end or the OV-CC. But let us watch each other's back just in case help is needed."

Nathan gave Joshua a thumbs up and said, "Let's go and good luck!"

Joshua has an assault rifle taken from one of the two men he killed earlier with a shot between the eyes. Along with the rifle he also carries two clips with 25 rounds of ammo each. In addition, he has the pistol he took from the guard earlier. Nathan, on the other hand, has his remaining 10 star weapons.

On the way out, Joshua fired at the rear tires of the OV-OE to prevent it from escaping. This triggered the opening of machine gun windows at the rear end and two sides of the OV-OE. When Nathan saw the gun barrels on the OV-OE scanning for targets, he immediately grabbed and with Super Ring force pulled them out before they could fire any shots and become hot. Nathan heard rifle shots inside the OV-OE hitting the rear machine gun mount. He opened a side door and entered the vehicle simultaneously rolling on the floor. A startled security staff fired at him but missed. Nathan threw a star weapon and hit the man on the chest. He slumped on the floor dead facing up. Nathan pulled the dead body out of the passage way. When Nathan heard hasty footsteps, he stood by one side of the door and waited. Upon emerging at the door, Nathan tripped the enemy with his foot and simultaneously whacked his back. The man fell down right over the dead security staff. The other edge of the star weapon on the dead man's chest penetrated the stomach of the falling man that Nathan tripped. He too died instantly over the first dead man.

Nathan then heard the clicking of a rifle magazine being loaded. He sensed someone was going to fire random shots toward the door. As rapidly as he could, Nathan ducked on the floor under an operating table until the haphazard firing ceased. At extraordinary speed, Nathan rushed toward the man in green medical uniform, grabbed the rifle and head butted him. The man fell on the floor unconscious. Nathan dashed back to the OV-SQ, took out handcuffs and quickly returned to the OV-OE.

Suddenly, two middle-age nurses in green medical uniforms showed up with hands over their heads. Nathan handcuffed the two nurses as well as the unconscious man and tied them on one of the operating tables.

At the OV-CC, Joshua fired at the rear of the vehicle prompting it to open the machine gun window. When it did, he successively fired several shots at its mount and at the telescope used in controlling the gun. This disabled the machine gun at the rear of the vehicle. He then killed one man inside by shooting him through the gun port when he saw a still-smoking gun barrel pulled out of the port after an indiscriminate firing to the outside.

Joshua crept facing upward under the vehicle and cautiously listened to footsteps on the floor over him. When he heard hurried footsteps directly above his location, he fired repeatedly upward hitting the person directly above. Since Joshua did not know how thick and hard the vehicle floor is, he made sure that some bullets went through the floor with deadly velocity by repeating shots at particular points. The first shot softened the point, if not actually penetrating it. This made it easier for the second shot to go through and kill the person above. Joshua killed the remaining three men inside the vehicle in this manner.

Coming out from under the vehicle, Joshua cautiously entered it just in case there were more security personnel inside. He found no one else inside except the dead bodies of the four men he just killed. Joshua then disabled the radio control system for the machine gun at the rear.

Nathan was on his way to the OV-CC just as Joshua alighted from it. They embraced each other with great joy.

IN STEALTH MODE 20

Since receiving Nathan's message through Deputy Sturgess about the organ chopper carrying the foreign doctors, the Black Hawk helicopter has switched to stealth mode to avoid radar detection along its path or from other aircraft. Blimps were now showing on the Black Hawk's radar screen. Agent Stern believed these could be the organ chopper since it was flying toward the same destination as the Black Hawk. He told his pilot to closely monitor its path. "We do not want to lose sight of this aircraft. This is an important object for us."

At the organ chopper, the syndicate's boss was worried that he was not getting any messages from the OV-SC despite his repeated efforts to contact. He talked to the pilot about the possibility of diverting destination if things were not right at their present camp. But first they have to see what had happened in the camp.

"Sir, visual contact with destination at 12 o'clock." The Black Hawk pilot informed Agent Stern.

Agent Stern replied, "Make a fly over the site to let them know we have arrived. But we will not land since we have to wait for the organ chopper and prevent it from getting away. We have to force it to land and arrest the passengers."

"Got it, Sir," the pilot responded.

During a wide turn after passing the site, the Black Hawk pilot told Agent Stern. "Visual contact with the organ chopper, Sir at 3:00 o'clock."

"Do you think they have seen us?" Agent Stern inquired.

Pilot to Agent Stern, "I don't think so, Sir. They have not changed their flight direction."

"Increase altitude so that we will be on top of them. We can then move closer without being seen until we are close enough to signal them to land. But contact the pilot first through the common frequency." Agent Stern instructed the pilot.

"Roger, Sir," the pilot acknowledged. Almost instantly the Black Hawk hovered about 200 feet over the organ chopper. It then started to inch toward the organ chopper, which up to now had maintained its flight direction.

"Chopper 485, this is FBI Black Hawk, do you copy? Over." The Black Hawk pilot asked through the common radio frequency. There was no reply.

When the Black Hawk was about 100 feet away, the pilot and passengers of the organ chopper must have seen it because they got agitated and the chopper started to alter its flight path.

Quickly maneuvering closer, the Black Hawk pilot called again. "Chopper 485, this is FBI Black Hawk, come in 485. We want you to land your chopper. Do you copy 485?" Since there was no reply, one FBI agent hand signaled the organ chopper to land.

Instead of following the radioed instructions to land, the organ chopper pilot on orders of the syndicate boss evaded the Black Hawk and attempted a getaway. The Black Hawk anticipated the organ chopper's move and blocked its way. By now the two helicopters are over the camp.

The Black Hawk continued to inch closer to the organ chopper while instructing it again to land. When the organ chopper tried another getaway maneuver, Agent Stern ordered the Black Hawk gunner, "Since it won't follow our command, give that chopper a kiss."

"Roger, Sir." The Black Hawk gunner acknowledged. He then aimed and locked one machine gun located under the Black Hawk's belly toward the nose of the organ chopper then fired two shots. The organ chopper was jolted when it was hit at the front belly injuring the syndicate boss' right foot.

The two foreign doctors on board were extremely aggravated and apprehensive. "You did not tell us this would happen. Land this chopper now!"

Both choppers landed on the abandoned helipad. The FBI agents arrested all those on board the other chopper.

THANK YOU, EAGLE SPIRIT 21

Joshua and Nathan rushed to meet Agent Stern. It was a happy reunion between two former long-time war buddies now FBI Special Agent William Stern and Camanor Chief of Police Joshua Dean. Joshua then introduced Nathan to Agent Stern. For Nathan shaking the hand of the man he has long admired based on his father's account of their exploits in the Iran war and the photographs displayed in the Dean's household was an exceptionally memorable moment.

Edgar, together with the other freed victims approached Joshua and told him everyone was well and anxious to get home. Agent Stern informed Joshua that as soon as he received Nathan's message that everyone had been rescued unharmed, he contacted the nearest FBI district office and requested for a bus to take the rescued victims home. He also asked to contact the local police to come and process the organ syndicate personnel.

Agent Stern subsequently told Joshua that there was enough space for him and Nathan in the Black Hawk if they prefer to be dropped off at Camanor on his way back to Washington, D.C. Joshua thanked him but declined as he wanted to be with the rescued victims. Instead Joshua warmly and gratefully told Agent Stern. "We should plan to camp together with our families one of these days."

Agent Stern gladly replied. "Great idea. Indeed we should! I will keep in touch about it and other important matters on this case."

There was intense conversation about how horrible the crime that this group was doing. Agent Stern mentioned that they have received tips about its earlier operation in the East. However, the FBI and the local police have been unable to arrest any of those involved because they just disappeared from the area. The syndicate had moved its operation to Camanor.

Unknown to everybody, a bloodied individual, who could have just been unconscious in the earlier explosions at the OV-SC had recovered and found his way up to the opening used for repair and maintenance of radar and satellite antennae on the roof of the vehicle. He carried a machine gun and was about to fire at the crowd. Suddenly Eagle Spirit made a screeching sound while simultaneously attacking the man atop the OV-SC, momentarily foiling his attempt to fire at the group of people nearby. At exactly the same instant, Agent Stern and Joshua fired their pistols at the man, who was then hit twice on the forehead. The man lost his grip on the machine gun and fell inside the vehicle. Upon seeing the machine gun falling from atop the vehicle, Nathan using his Super-Ring endowed speed rushed toward it and caught the gun before hitting the ground and avoided an uncontrollable firing that could hit anyone in the group. Everyone heaved a big sigh of relief.

Nathan then turned toward the big tree where Eagle Spirit was perched. "Thank you, Eagle Spirit, thank you!"

Eagle Spirit flapped his wings in acknowledgment.

In unison, all the kidnapped victims led by the charming fourth grader, Amy, said loudly. "Thank you, Eagle Spirit. We are very grateful."

Eagle Spirit left his perch and looped around several times over the crowd showing off his brilliant plumage in recognition of the gratitude expressed by the kidnapped victims. He then ascended into the blue mid-morning sky and gradually disappeared in the horizon.

THE END

APPENDICES

Appendix A—Platinum

Platinum is an extremely rare metal with a concentration of only 0.0005 ppm in the earth's crust. Pure platinum is silver-white in color, lustrous and more ductile than gold, silver and copper. It is heavier than gold with a higher density of 21.45 g/cm³ compared to gold's 19.32 g/cm³.

Aside from its popular use as jewelry, platinum is used in catalytic converters, laboratory equipment, electrical contacts, platinum resistance thermometers, electrodes and dentistry equipment. Because only a few hundred tons are produced annually, it is a scarce material, highly valuable and a major precious metal commodity. South Africa produces the most amount of platinum. Columbia, South America and the Ural Mountains, Russia are also important sources. This metal is believed to be abundant on the moon and in meteorites.

Compounds containing platinum, most notably cisplatin, are applied in chemotherapy to treat certain types of cancer. Pure platinum is slightly harder than pure iron. The metal has an excellent resistance to corrosion and high temperature and has stable electrical properties. All these characteristics are important in various industries.

Because of its scarcity and broad industrial use, platinum is more expensive than gold. As of early 2014, platinum was priced at US$1435 per ounce compared with gold at US$1250 per ounce.

Comparative Physical Properties	Platinum	Gold	Iron
Melting Point	1768.3 °C	1064.18 °C	1538 °C
	3214.9 °F	1947.52 °F	2800 °F
	2041.0 K	1337.33 K	1811 K
Boiling Point	3825 °C	2856 °C	2861°C
	6917 °F	5173 °F	5182 °F
	4098 K	3129 K	3134 K
Density of Solid	21.45 g/cm^3	19.32 g/cm^3	7.87 g/cm^3

Source:

Kelly, Thomas D. and Matoos, Grecia R. (2013). Historical Statistics for Mineral and Material Commodities in the United States, U.S. Geological Survey

www.WebElements.com

Appendix B—Rare Earth Elements

There are 17 so-called rare earth elements (REEs). These elements are not really rare. They abundantly occur on the earth's crust. What makes them rare is the difficulty in separating them from surrounding rock which requires complex process involving a host of chemical compounds that have serious environmental impact. Up until the 1990s, most of the rare earth elements came from the United States, especially Mountain Pass, a mine in California near Los Angeles, which supplied most of the late 1960s europium demand. Since Mountain Pass closed in 2003, the United States ceased to be a supplier of the metal. While the U.S. still has plenty of rare earth elements left to mine in Mountain Pass and elsewhere, it was undercut on price by Chinese companies that had lower labor costs and lax environmental policies. The Chinese also benefited from their mining of rare earth elements as a byproduct of profitable iron mining. Currently, China supplies nearly 97 percent of rare earth elements used in several industries.

Because REEs have become important as we transition from carbon-based economy to the 21st century electron economy, they became vital in many industries. REEs are crucial to the way we live now. They made possible miniaturizing computers and headphones, smart phones and in powering hybrid vehicles as well as the manufacture of light, high-performance batteries.

Popular Mechanics magazine identified four out of the 17 rare earth elements that are expected to get increasingly more important, namely:

a) Lanthanum – First discovered in 1893, there is actually more lanthanum on earth than silver or lead and it is the second most abundant rare earth element. However, there were no uses for it in the early days. Up until the late 1970s and early 1980s, lanthanum mostly went into stockpiles, waiting for the day when it could be sold off for higher prices. That day has come. Today, unknown to its owners, every Prius and other hybrid cars carry with them about 10 pounds of lanthanum. This comes in its battery called "nickel-metal hydride." The metal component of such battery is actually lanthanum. This big breakthrough in battery technology, i.e., nickel-lanthanum hydride batteries provide about twice the efficiency as the standard lead-acid car battery and enabled manufacturers to pack more power into a smaller space.

b) Europium – As reported in *Popular Mechanics* Magazine, europium was the first isolated, high purity rare earth element to enter the public marketplace in 1967 as a source of the color red in television sets. Although there had been color televisions before europium, the color quality was weak as the sets relied on phosphors – substances that glow when struck with electrons or other energized particles – to get their red, green and blue colors. Early red phosphors could not produce a very bright color. The use of europium phosphors made the picture bright.

Europium is expected to show up in white LED-based lights, an energy-efficient replacement for both incandescent and compact fluorescent bulbs. This technology involves mixing various colored LEDs and europium red happens to be an ingredient in turning out a high-quality, attractive shade of white.

c) Erbium – The only way to create a stable pink shade in glass is to add erbium. Thus, erbium-doped glass shows up in novelty sunglasses and decorator vases. But the more important uses of erbium are in fiber optic technology as well as in infrared lasers. Adding a little erbium to the optical fibers that carry data around the globe in the form of light pulses amplifies those pulses. Likewise it can also be used as part of the gain medium that amplifies light in lasers. With this, you end up with a laser that can be used for dental surgery and skin treatment because it does not build up much heat in the human skin it is pointed at.

Erbium typifies how rare earth elements work in practical applications whereby a single chunk is not being used. Instead, small doses are added to composites and alloys. The unique chemical and physical properties of rare earth elements allow them to interact with other elements and get results that neither element could get on its own.

d) Neodymium – This rare earth element is responsible for miniaturizing most of everyday gadgetry used in our daily lives from hard drives to headphones to anything that incorporates a small electric motor. The key is magnets. In the past, producing a strong magnetic field used to require a big, heavy magnet and thus led to big pieces of technology. This dramatically changed with the introduction of magnets made first with rare earth samarium then later replaced with neodymium, which are much smaller and even stronger.

Magnets with neodymium are likewise responsible for making necessarily chunky technology lighter and cheaper such as the turbines in wind farms that turn wind into electricity, and the drills that search for oil deep below the Earth's surface.

Source/Reference:
4 Rare Earth Elements That Will Only Get More Important – *Popular Mechanics,* www.PopularMechanics.com, 01/12/2014

Appendix C—Plasma Gasification

Plasma arc waste destruction systems employ plasma gasification whereby waste materials are converted into synthetic gas or fuel without producing emissions. This innovative technology is now finding its way into areas having serious household waste disposal problem.

Essentially, plasma gasification begins with a furnace heated to 1,500°F where waste materials are fed and mixed with oxygen and steam. The resulting chemical reaction vaporizes 75 to 85 percent of the waste, transforming it into a blend of gases known as syngas, which is piped out of the system and segregated. This can be used to create synthetic natural gas. The remaining substances that are still chemically intact, move to another smaller chamber with two electrodes inside that create an electric arc almost as hot as lightning at 18,000°F. The intense and sustained energy becomes so hot it enables reactions to take place at more than 2,700°F resulting in molecular deconstruction of the materials, i.e. transformation of materials into their constituent atomic elements. The process is emission-free because the waste material is blasted apart by plasma, the so-called fourth state of matter.

A plasma gasification system is energy-intensive. In actual practice though, the syngas produced can power the plasma torches making the system self-sustaining. Places now operating a plasma gasification system or have shown interest in installing the system includes Columbia Ridge and Arlington, Oregon; McCarran, Nevada; New York City, U.S.A; Utashinai City, Japan and Morcenx, France. A plasma gasification system has been hard at work at Hurlburt Field Air Force base in Florida's panhandle. On the other hand, the U.S. Navy is employing Plasma Arc Waste Destruction System (PAWDS) on its latest generation of Gerald R. Ford-class aircraft carrier. The compact system is designed to treat all combustible solid waste generated on board the ship. After completing factory acceptance testing in Montreal, Canada, the system will be shipped to the Huntington Ingalls shipyard for installation on the carrier.

Sources/References:
http://www.en.wikipedia.org/wiki/Plasma_gasification
http://www.wired.com/magazine/2012/ff_trashblaster
http://nytimes.com/2012/09/11/science/
plasma_gasification

Appendix D—Bloom's Energy Server

Bloom energy is generated using a patented solid oxide fuel cell (SOFC) technology whereby fuel cell devices convert fuel into electricity through a clean electro-chemical process. Because SOFCs operate at extremely high temperatures, normally exceeding 1400°F, very high efficiencies in electrical generation are obtained. It also allows for fuel use flexibility, which could either be renewable or fossil-based. Using the combined low-cost ceramic materials with extremely high electrical efficiencies of the process enables the continuous production of low-cost, emission-free electrical energy.

Bloom's Energy Server (BES) is a new class of distributed power generators, producing emission-free and affordable electricity at point of consumption with high reliability. Distributed generation refers to power generation at the point of use or on-site that eliminates the cost, complexity and inefficiencies associated with electric transmission and distribution.

Each Energy Server consists of thousands of Bloom fuel cells, which are flat, solid ceramic squares made from a common sand-like 'powder' material. A Bloom Energy fuel cell is capable of producing 25W of electricity. For more power, the cells are sandwiched with metal interconnecting plates into a fuel cell 'stack'.

Several stacks together that are about the size of a loaf bread are sufficient to power an average home.

In an Energy Server, several stacks are aggregated into a power module and then into multiple power modules along with a common fuel input and electrical output to form a complete system. Where more power is required, multiple Energy Servers can be deployed side by side. This modular Energy Server architecture provides easy and fast deployment, inherent redundancy for fault tolerance, higher power availability since one module can be serviced while all others continue to operate, and most importantly, mobility.

Source:

http://www.bloomenergy.com
01/10/2014